SMUGG

'You keep away from that middle path,' said the man.

'Why?' asked Peter.

The man's face grew dark. 'That's the cliff path. It's dangerous,' he said. 'That's why. You don't want to go getting hurt, do you?'

Holly looked at him. He had small narrow eyes and she thought there was a threat in his tone of voice.

'Go on,' he said. 'Get out of it. And don't you be coming back here again.'

'We're going,' said Peter.

'And mind what I said about those cliffs,' said the man. 'We don't want any accidents, do we?'

Holly looked round sharply. That definitely *did* sound like a threat.

The Mystery Kids series

THE MYSTERY KIDS
Smugglers Bay

Fiona Kelly

Dean
oentles

Hodder
Children's
Books

a division of Hodder Headline plc

Special thanks to Helen Magee

Copyright © 1995 Ben M. Baglio
Created by Ben M. Baglio
London W6 0HE

First published in Great Britain in 1995
by Hodder Children's Books

A Catalogue record for this book is
available from the British Library

ISBN 0 340 61993 7

Typeset by Hewer Text Composition Services, Edinburgh
Printed and bound in Great Britain by
Cox & Wyman Ltd, Reading, Berkshire

Hodder Children's Books
A division of Hodder Headline plc
338 Euston Road
London NW1 3BH

Contents

# 1 An exciting phone call

The sun streaming in the little window was as hot as ever.

'This must be the hottest summer ever,' Miranda Hunt said, pushing her long blonde hair back for the hundredth time.

'London gets so hot and sticky,' said Holly Adams. 'What I wouldn't give for a cool sea breeze.'

'Some chance,' said Peter Hamilton.

The Mystery Kids were in their office – a boxroom wedged between two bedrooms in Peter's house. Peter's dad had been really good about letting them have it.

Holly looked round the room. It was tiny – too tiny for the three of them on a hot day like this. But it was *theirs*; their very own office.

Miranda slumped back on a cushion and looked at the big map of London on the wall. 'And the only mystery we've got is

Mrs Griebler's earring,' she said with disgust.

Holly stuck a red pin in the map to mark her next door neighbour's house.

'But it *is* mysterious,' she said. 'Mrs Griebler is sure she left her earring on the windowsill. And when she came back it was gone.'

Peter grinned. 'What a come down,' he said. 'We've foiled bank robbers and caught thieves and now we're looking for an earring.'

Holly perched herself on the edge of Miranda's cushion and looked up at Peter. 'It's important to Mrs Griebler,' she said, hugging her legs.

'OK,' said Peter. 'Let's go over the clues. Mrs Griebler left the earring on the windowsill.'

'Nobody else was in the house,' said Holly.

'What about the garden?' said Miranda.

Holly shook her shoulder-length brown hair back. 'Nobody,' she said. 'Mrs Griebler was alone.'

Miranda sighed. 'It's so hot, I can't think,' she said.

'What would Harriet the Spy make of it?' Holly said.

2

The Mystery Kids read all the mystery books they could get their hands on. But *Harriet the Spy* was their favourite.

'Maybe it was a cat burglar,' said Peter.

Miranda sat up. 'Maybe he came over the roof and swung down on a rope to the kitchen window.'

'Just for an earring?' said Holly.

Miranda frowned. 'Maybe it's special and Mrs Griebler doesn't know it,' she said.

Holly laughed. 'Mr Griebler bought them at Jones the Jeweller – in Highgate.'

'But unknown to Mr Griebler they aren't silver – they're platinum and really valuable,' said Miranda.

'And Mr Jones sold them by mistake,' said Peter.

'And turned himself into a cat burglar to get them back,' said Miranda.

'One of them,' said Holly. 'The other one was still there.'

'Oh!' said Peter, looking downcast. 'I'd forgotten that.'

He shoved his hair out of his eyes. Peter's hair was always falling over his eyes. Peter, Holly and Miranda sat in silence, thinking hard. They were used to mysteries. They were good at solving them. That's why they called themselves the Mystery Kids.

Downstairs the phone began to ring. Peter made for the door.

'I bet that's Interpol,' said Miranda at once. 'They need our help to catch a gang of international jewel thieves.'

'It's probably my mum,' Holly said glumly. 'Wanting me to go and get a new school uniform.'

'Only ten days till we go back to school,' said Miranda as they listened to Peter leaping down the stairs two at a time.

'And all we'll have to write about is Mrs Griebler's earring,' said Holly.

'If we find it,' said Miranda.

Holly and Miranda edited the lower school magazine, *The Tom-tom*. They wrote a mystery column for it. Miranda also wrote a bad jokes column but Peter and Holly tried not to remind her about that. She was always trying her jokes out on them.

Holly and Miranda heard Peter's feet on the stairs and the door swung open.

'You aren't going to believe this,' he said.

'It *was* Interpol?' said Miranda sitting up.

Peter shook his head. 'It wasn't Interpol,'

he said. 'It was Dad. He has to go away on business.'

Mr Hamilton was an architect. He and Peter lived alone. Peter's mother had died when he was little.

'What about you?' said Holly.

Peter shrugged. 'He says he can't leave me here on my own. So I have to go too.'

'What a shame,' said Miranda. 'Boring old business.'

Peter looked thoughtful. 'It might not be too bad,' he said. 'Dad's been asked to take over the design of a conservatory at a big house in Cornwall.'

'Sounds exciting,' Holly said doubtfully.

Peter laughed. 'It's by the sea,' he said.

Holly and Miranda looked at him, their jaws dropping.

'That's amazing,' said Miranda. 'We were just talking about going to the seaside.' She narrowed her eyes. 'Are you sure you haven't got psychic powers or something?'

Peter closed his eyes and began to sway about. 'I see an earring,' he said, clutching his head. 'It's hazy. Where is it?' He opened his eyes and grinned. 'Nope, the vision's gone,' he said.

'How long are you going for?' Holly said.

'A week,' said Peter.

'Lucky you,' Miranda sighed. 'I wish we could go too. Just think of it – a whole week at the seaside.'

Peter looked at the girls. 'Do you want to come?' he said.

Holly and Miranda looked at each other. '*Do* we?' they said together.

Peter grinned. 'I thought you would,' he said. 'So I asked Dad if we could all go.'

'That would be terrific!' Miranda said.

'But it's a business trip,' said Holly. 'He can't go dragging all of us off with him.'

Peter shrugged. 'Oh, I don't know,' he said. 'It sounds as if the house is pretty big and Dad says there was no problem about me going. What difference does another two make? He says he'll get in touch with the client and ring back.'

'Wow!' said Miranda. 'A week at the seaside. Who says wishes don't come true?'

'We aren't there yet,' said Holly, then she swung round. 'That's the phone, Peter.'

Peter was already halfway out of the door. They heard his feet pounding on the stairs and went to hang over the banister as he took the call.

'What's he saying?' Miranda whispered.

'I can't hear,' said Holly, straining her ears.

Then Peter came pounding up the stairs, his face alight.

'It's OK,' he said. 'Dad phoned Mr Allenbury. We can all go. The house is huge.' He paused. 'And it has its own private beach.'

'What?' screeched Miranda. 'This Mr Allenbury must be rich.'

'What is he, a millionaire?' said Holly.

'Or an international crook?' said Miranda.

'He's just a nice guy,' said Peter. Then he wrinkled his nose.

'What is it?' said Holly. 'There's a drawback.'

'It's a mad housekeeper who'll lock us in an attic,' said Miranda. 'Or an insane butler?'

'Don't be daft,' Peter said, laughing. 'It's only that Mr Allenbury has a daughter. He thinks we'll be good company for her.'

'What's so bad about that?' said Holly.

'She's probably spoiled rotten,' said

Miranda. 'She probably doesn't have any friends of her own.'

'She's only seven,' said Peter.

Holly and Miranda looked at each other.

'That's even younger than Jamie,' Holly said. Jamie was Holly's little brother and a real pest.

'At least she's a girl,' Miranda said. 'Even if she is five years younger than us.'

'Hey, wait a minute,' Peter said. 'What do you mean by that?'

Miranda giggled. 'Whoops! Nothing, Peter. Honestly!' she said.

Peter ran a hand through his brown hair. 'I just don't know what we're supposed to do with a seven year old girl. She'll be a real nuisance.' He frowned. 'She'll probably want to play with dolls and stuff.' He looked determined. 'I am *not* playing dolls with her,' he said firmly.

But Miranda wasn't listening. 'Who cares?' she said. 'We're going away. Out of sticky old Highgate. I don't care if she *is* spoiled rotten and a complete pest. We're off to the seaside!'

'If our parents let us,' said Holly.

'Oh, they won't mind,' said Miranda airily.

Then she laughed loudly. 'My mum will be glad to get some peace and quiet.'

Holly smiled. *That* she could believe.

'When are we going?' she said.

Peter grinned. 'Tomorrow.'

'Cripes,' said Holly. 'We'd better get moving on Mrs Griebler's mystery then.'

Miranda looked at her. 'Who cares about an old earring?' she said. 'We're off to Cornwall, to a millionaire's house full of mad butlers and dotty housekeepers.' She looked from Peter to Holly, her eyes shining. 'And I just bet we'll find a better mystery in Cornwall than Mrs Griebler's earring.'

Holly was still thinking about Mrs Griebler's earring when her mother called up to tell her Mr Hamilton was on his way to pick her up.

'Coming, Mum,' she shouted as she pushed a few last-minute things into her rucksack. Her very own police notebook was already packed. Inspector Simmonds at the local police station had given Holly, Peter and Miranda a notebook each when they had caught a pair of thieves. Holly used hers to record clues for all the Mystery Kids' investigations. She looked round her bed-room and picked up a pocket torch and shoved it on top of the already bulging rucksack. You never knew when a mystery would appear and it was best to be prepared.

'Ready to go,' she said to the empty room.

It had taken a bit of explaining and a phone call to Mr Hamilton before Mrs Adams had agreed to let her go off to Cornwall. But now everything was arranged. Almost everything. There was still Mrs Griebler's earring.

Holly looked out of the window at the fence that separated their garden from the Grieblers'. She smiled as she saw a couple of magpies squabbling on the lawn. *One for sorrow, two for joy*, she thought. *That's a good omen*.

Then she stopped, her mouth open. That was it. That was what had happened to Mrs Griebler's earring.

Holly turned and raced downstairs.

'Back in a minute, Mum,' she called to Mrs Adams. 'I've just got to pop over to the Grieblers.'

'Don't be long — ' Mrs Adams started to say. But Holly was running out of the door, long legs flying.

'I won't,' Holly called back over her shoulder. 'I've just solved a mystery!'

 **Greystones**

'And it was a magpie?' Miranda said.

Holly had just finished telling her about solving Mrs Griebler's mystery. Miranda had been talking so much it was hard to get a word in. She had stayed up half the night reading a book about Cornwall and smugglers. She was full of stories about shipwrecks and pirates.

Now they were well into Cornwall, travelling along lanes bordered by high hedges.

Holly nodded. 'I'd been watching those magpies for days. I just hadn't thought. Magpies are attracted to bright things. They pick them up and hide them in their nests.'

'But how can you be sure it was the magpies?' Miranda said.

Holly shrugged. 'It was just so obvious – once I connected the two things. I mean, why would anybody steal just one earring? And there was nobody around at the time.'

'So what did Mrs Griebler say?' said Miranda.

Holly giggled. 'She said Mr Griebler would have to climb up and get it,' she said.

Peter squirmed round in his seat. 'He'll probably find loads of other shiny things as well,' he said. 'Magpies are really clever that way.' He patted a case slung round his neck. 'I've brought my binoculars. I want to do a bit of bird-watching.'

'Seabirds,' said Miranda. 'I can't wait to have a swim.'

'Me too,' said Holly. They had been in the car for hours and Holly felt really hot and sticky.

'Nearly there,' said Mr Hamilton from the driving seat. 'Look for the turn-off, Peter.'

Peter bent over the map. 'It should be on the right. We must be pretty close now,' he said.

Holly and Miranda turned to look out of the car windows. Suddenly, the tall green hedges gave way to bright blue sky and there was the sea.

'Wow!' said Miranda. 'What a brilliant view!'

The sea glittered in the late afternoon sun.

'I could jump right in,' said Peter.

14

Mr Hamilton laughed. 'Not just yet,' he said. 'I think this might be where we're headed.'

Up in front was a pair of stone pillars with wide gates standing open. The name of the house was picked out in stone lettering on one of the pillars.

'Greystones,' said Holly. She shivered. 'It sounds spooky.'

'Cripes,' said Peter. 'It must be even bigger than we thought.'

The drive swept round in an arc, bordered by trees. The car emerged from the trees and the front of the house came into view. Miranda and Holly gasped. Even Mr Hamilton drew in his breath.

'It's enormous!' said Holly.

'Like a castle!' said Miranda.

Peter just sat with his mouth open.

'I can see why it will take a week to design the conservatory,' Mr Hamilton said. 'If that's the size of the house, the conservatory must be pretty big.'

The car stopped and Holly turned to Peter. Peter wasn't looking at the house now. He was looking towards the sea.

'Look at that,' he said.

Broad lawns swept down towards a flight of stone steps.

'That must be the way down to the beach,' said Mr Hamilton. 'Look! You can just see a path going off to the left at the bottom of the steps.'

'Our own private beach,' said Holly.

'I didn't think it would be as grand as this,' said Peter.

Miranda shook her head as they got out of the car. 'Mr Allenbury must be *really* rich,' she said.

There was a sound of barking and a little terrier appeared at the front door of the house. Behind him was a girl. She had bright red hair tied up in bunches with blue ribbons. She bent and picked up the dog, cuddling it to her cheek.

'He doesn't bite,' she said. 'I'm Lucy.' She shook her head and her bunches danced. 'I've got new hair ribbons.'

'They're terrific,' said Miranda, grinning.

Holly looked at the little girl. She was wearing scruffy old shorts and a striped T-shirt. Her eyes were blue and bright with excitement. Holly smiled at her. She didn't look in the least spoiled.

16

'I'm Miranda Hunt,' Miranda said. Then she grinned. 'What's your dog called?'

Lucy grinned back. 'Rags,' she said. 'Do you like dogs?'

Peter smiled and went forward to pat Rags. 'Love them,' he said. 'Especially terriers.'

Lucy smiled up at him, her face glowing.

Holly and Miranda looked at each other.

'We don't have to worry about her being spoiled,' Holly whispered.

Miranda grinned, then rolled her eyes. 'All we have to worry about are the mad butlers and dotty housekeepers.'

There was a flurry of movement at the door and a voice said. 'Hallo. I'm Mrs Trelawny, the housekeeper.'

Miranda choked and tried to look as if she had never mentioned housekeepers – dotty or otherwise.

Holly grinned, then almost choked herself. Mrs Trelawny was carrying a large feather duster in one hand and a turnip in the other. Maybe she *was* dotty after all.

Mrs Trelawny smiled. 'Don't worry, I'm not dusting the turnip,' she said, her eyes twinkling.

'Daddy!' Lucy cried.

Mrs Trelawny looked across the lawns. 'Here's Mr Allenbury now,' she said.

Holly turned round. A tall dark-haired man in green corduroy trousers and an open-necked shirt was walking across the lawns. He was talking to another man who was shorter and had untidy sandy-coloured hair. As Holly watched, the tall man said something sharply to the other man who turned away, walking back down towards the sea. As he went, he turned his head and looked at the group by the door. Holly shivered. It wasn't a very nice look.

'Smugglers,' Miranda whispered in her ear.

'Don't be daft,' Holly whispered back.

Miranda gave her a wait-and-see look, narrowing her eyes. Holly sighed. Some day Miranda's imagination would get her into real trouble.

Lucy was running to the tall man. 'Daddy,' she said. 'They're here.'

Mr Allenbury swung her up into his arms and came towards them smiling. He was very tanned and with his white open-necked shirt he *did* look a bit like a pirate. Holly gave herself a shake. She was getting as bad as Miranda.

Mr Hamilton shook hands with him and the two men began to talk about the conservatory.

'It's in a bad way,' Mr Allenbury said. 'I only bought the house a few months ago but I want the conservatory restored to its former glory. I hope it isn't asking too much.'

Mr Hamilton smiled. 'Let's go and have a look at it,' he said. He turned to Peter. 'What are you going to do?'

Holly, Peter and Miranda looked at one another. 'Swim!' they all said together.

Mr Allenbury laughed. 'Good idea,' he said. 'Why don't you let Mrs Trelawny show you where you're sleeping, then you can have a swim.' He paused and frowned. 'You can all swim, can't you?' he said.

Holly, Peter and Miranda nodded.

'Just be careful,' Mr Allenbury went on. 'The cliffs can be dangerous. Don't go too near them.'

'We won't,' said Peter as Mr Allenbury and Mr Hamilton strode off round the side of the house.

'Can I go with them?' Lucy said to Mrs Trelawny.

Mrs Trelawny shook her head. 'You know your daddy thinks you're too young to go down to the beach without him.'

Lucy's lip trembled.

'We'll bring you back some shells,' Holly said and the little girl smiled.

'And I'll show you where your rooms are,' she said. 'They're near my room.'

Mrs Trelawny straightened her apron briskly. 'When you've unpacked, come down to the kitchen,' she said. 'You must be starving.'

'You bet,' said Peter.

'How can you be hungry?' said Holly. 'We stopped for burgers less than an hour ago.'

'Hollow legs,' said Miranda. 'Peter is always hungry.'

'Then he's come to the right place,' Mrs Trelawny said. 'I like a boy with a good appetite.' She looked at Peter's lanky figure. 'He looks as if he could do with feeding up.'

'He's a bottomless pit,' Holly said warningly. 'But it would be nice to have something after our swim.'

Mrs Trelawny laughed. 'Don't worry, Peter,' she said. 'I'll give you double helpings.'

Peter looked smug and Miranda gave him a dig in the ribs.

'Come on!' Lucy shouted from inside the house, and Rags gave a short bark.

'Coming,' said Holly and the three of them followed Lucy into the house.

'My room's terrific,' said Peter as he came into the girls' room.

'So is this,' said Miranda. 'You can see the sea from the windows.'

Holly and Miranda had unpacked as fast as possible and put their swimsuits on under shorts and T-shirts. Their room was big and airy with two single beds, a couple of chests of drawers and an enormous wardrobe.

'That wardrobe is nearly as big as my room at home,' Miranda said.

Lucy watched the three older children. 'Tomorrow, I'll show you the *whole* house,' she said. 'We've got even bigger wardrobes than that.'

Holly and Miranda laughed. 'You can show us everything,' Holly said.

Rags began to bark and Lucy bent down

and patted him. 'Mrs Trelawny wants me,' she said.

Holly looked at her in amazement. 'How do you know?' she said.

Lucy put her head on one side. 'Rags knows,' she said. 'Rags is very clever,' and she skipped out of the room with Rags at her heels.

'Great kid,' said Peter.

'Great dog,' said Miranda.

'Great place,' said Holly. 'Let's go swimming!'

They clattered downstairs and out into the sunlit afternoon.

'Dad was telling me Lucy's mum died in a car crash five years ago,' Peter said as they made their way across the lawns towards the steps.

Holly and Miranda gave each other a quick glance. Peter and Lucy had something in common. Peter was so young when his mum died, he didn't even remember her.

'Poor Lucy,' Holly said.

Peter nodded. 'She's a good kid,' he said.

Miranda and Holly exchanged another look and smiled. Lucy was definitely *not* going to be a nuisance to Peter.

'There are three paths,' said Miranda as they reached the bottom of the steps.

The Mystery Kids looked at the paths.

Holly shrugged. 'Let's take the nearest one,' she said.

'Might as well,' said Miranda as she set off along the first path.

But after a little while, Holly wasn't so sure they had chosen correctly.

'It goes through a wood,' she said, pointing.

'It looks pretty dark in there,' said Miranda. 'I don't think this path has been used in a long time.'

'Come on then, let's explore,' said Peter and plunged on ahead.

'Wait for us,' Holly shouted and the girls dived after him.

They caught up with him on the edge of a clearing in the wood.

'What a creepy place,' said Miranda.

'And look at that,' said Holly, pointing to a little wooden building in the centre of the clearing.

'What is it?' said Peter, puzzled.

Holly frowned as they made their way across the clearing towards it. Tall grasses

23

grew up all round the building. It had a pointed roof and windows with tiny panes of glass. Most of the glass had fallen out.

'It looks like the witch's house in *Hansel and Gretel*,' Miranda said.

'It's a summer-house,' Holly said.

'It would make a great Mystery Kids head-quarters,' Peter said.

'It would be perfect,' said Miranda. 'It's a shame we're only here for a week. Let's explore it.'

Peter kicked some dried leaves away from the door. 'It isn't locked,' he said, pulling the door open.

Holly peered in. There was a bench running round the walls and three cane chairs with moth-eaten cushions on them.

'Ugh!' said Miranda. 'It smells musty.'

'We could clean it up,' said Holly. 'I think Peter's idea is terrific.'

Holly, Peter and Miranda looked at one another. What a wonderful place for their headquarters.

'Now all we need is a mystery,' said Holly.

Miranda sniffed. 'I reckon we've got one already,' she said. 'I think that Mr Allenbury is a pretty suspicious character.'

'Why?' said Holly, lifting a cushion. Dust rose up and made her sneeze.

'Well, for one thing, what does he want with a great big house?'

Peter shrugged. 'He has to spend his money somehow.'

'Aha!' said Miranda.

'What do you mean, "Aha"?' said Holly.

Miranda narrowed her eyes. 'Where did he get his money? That's what I'd like to know.'

'Oh, Miranda—' Holly began but there was a shout from outside.

'Hoi! You kids. Get on out of there. What are you doing?'

Holly, Peter and Miranda filed out of the summer-house. The sandy-haired man they had seen talking to Mr Allenbury was standing there looking angry.

'We weren't doing any harm,' said Holly.

'We were only exploring,' Peter said.

'Don't give me that,' said the man. 'Exploring, is it? I'll give you exploring if I ever catch you here again. That there place is dangerous. You keep out of it, you hear me?'

Miranda put her nose in the air. 'We were

going swimming anyway,' she said. 'It's just a crummy old summer-house.'

'Swimming, is it?' said the man. 'Well, you've come the wrong way. You'll need to go back. There are three paths back there. It's the one furthest away you want. You keep away from that middle path.'

'Why?' said Peter.

The man's face grew dark. Holly drew back. 'Never you mind why,' he said. Then his face changed and he tried to smile. It didn't work very well. 'That's the cliff path. It's dangerous,' he said. 'That's why. You don't want to go getting hurt, do you?'

Holly looked at him. He had small narrow eyes and she thought there was a threat in his tone of voice.

'Go on,' he said. 'Get out of it. And don't you be coming back here again.'

'We're going,' said Peter as the three of them walked back across the clearing.

'And mind what I said about those cliffs,' said the man. 'We don't want any accidents, do we?'

Holly looked round sharply. That definitely *did* sound like a threat.

26

'What a horrible man,' Miranda said as they made their way back through the wood.

Holly looked at her. It wasn't like Miranda to be scared, but her voice sounded shaky.

'I wonder who he is,' said Peter.

Holly turned to look back. He was still watching them.

Holly was glad when they found the right path and came out on to the dunes that led to the beach. The man didn't seem so frightening out here.

'Now, I bet *he*'s a smuggler,' said Miranda, and Holly laughed. Miranda had made a quick recovery.

'In league with Mr Allenbury?' Holly suggested.

Miranda nodded. 'You saw them earlier,' she said. 'I bet that summer-house is where they stash their stuff.'

Peter hooted. 'Miranda, nobody has been in there for years. You saw those leaves piled up against the door.'

But Miranda shook her head. 'I tell you,' she said. 'There's something funny going on here.'

'Maybe there is,' said Peter, pulling off his T-shirt. 'But right now I don't care how many funny things are going on. Look at this beach!'

The girls looked. It was marvellous. The sand dunes sloped down to white sand and, a little way further along, cliffs towered up into the sky.

'I bet there are caves along there,' said Holly.

'Of course there are,' said Miranda. 'The whole of this coast is full of caves. That's why there were so many smugglers.' Her eyes sparkled. 'I wonder what that man is smuggling.'

'Gold,' said Peter.

'Treasure from old ships wrecked on the rocks,' said Miranda. 'I bet there have been loads of treasure-seekers here. I can see them now.' She dropped her voice to an eerie whisper. 'They would come at the dead of night, creeping down the beach with knives between their teeth. Swim out to the wrecks. Dive for treasure.' Her eyes became thoughtful. 'I wonder if he ever goes diving.'

Holly was pulling off her T-shirt. 'Who?' she said.

'The smuggler,' said Miranda. 'The guy that chased us away from the summer-house.

I think we ought to spy on him – see if he goes diving off the rocks.'

Holly looked at her. Far from being scared, Miranda was right back to normal.

'Later,' Holly said. 'Right now I want to swim.'

'Race you to the sea!' Peter shouted and took off down the beach.

'Wait for me,' Miranda cried, hopping about trying to get out of her shorts.

The three of them raced down the beach into the sea. As they plunged, splashing into the water, Holly thought she had never felt anything as wonderful. The sticky heat of London was behind them. There was a week of swimming and exploring in front of them.

Only one shadow crossed her mind. Just why had that man been so angry at them exploring a boring old summer-house? His words echoed in her ears: 'We don't want any accidents, do we?' That hadn't been a warning. It had been a threat.

A sound in the night

'And there really were smugglers around here?' said Miranda looking smug.

'Of course there were,' said Mrs Trelawny. 'And wreckers too. There are books about them in the library in this house.'

Holly, Peter and Miranda were sitting round the big wooden table in the kitchen, finishing off a wonderful late tea of fresh baked scones. They had worked up quite an appetite swimming, and Mrs Trelawny guessed they would be too tired to wait for dinner. 'Wreckers?' said Peter through a mouthful of floury scone. Mrs Trelawny nodded. 'They used to lure ships on to the rocks and rob them.'

'You mean, on purpose?' Holly said.

'Oh, they did it on purpose,' Mrs Trelawny said. 'There was all kinds of wickedness went on round here. And all along the Cornish coast.'

31

'And there are piskies too,' said Lucy.

Holly looked at the little girl sitting bright-eyed beside Mrs Trelawny. Rags was at her side as usual.

'You'd call them pixies,' said Mrs Trelawny. 'There's many a story about piskies.'

'But wreckers were *real*,' Miranda said.

Mrs Trelawny gave her a look and put her head on one side. 'And piskies aren't?' she said.

Holly opened her mouth and closed it again. Did Mrs Trelawny really believe in piskies? She looked at Lucy, wide-eyed and listening. Either Mrs Trelawny was saying that for Lucy's sake or Miranda was right. There really was a dotty housekeeper at Greystones.

'And does smuggling still go on?' Miranda said. 'I bet it does.'

Mrs Trelawny shook her head, her lips pursed. 'That I couldn't say,' she said. Then she nodded. 'But I wouldn't say it doesn't.'

Miranda gave Holly one of her I-told-you-so looks.

'We met a man in the woods,' Peter said.

Mrs Trelawny looked up sharply. 'What man?' she said.

'Sandy hair and not very friendly,' Holly said shortly.

Mrs Trelawny nodded. 'That'll be Jordan,' she said. 'Don't you have anything to do with him.'

'Why not?' said Peter.

But Mrs Trelawny just shook her head. 'Up to no good, that one is,' she said. 'And bad-tempered with it. You keep out of his way.' She pursed up her lips. 'I don't know what Mr Allenbury was thinking of – employing him.'

Miranda raised her eyebrows and looked at Peter and Holly.

'But what does he do here?' Peter said.

Mrs Trelawny sniffed. 'Calls himself the gardener,' she said. 'But if you ask me, it's little enough he knows about gardening.'

The kitchen clock chimed eight and Mrs Trelawny got up. 'My, my,' she said. 'That time already.' She turned to Lucy. 'Time for bed, young lady,' she said.

'Just five more minutes,' Lucy said.

Holly yawned and Mrs Trelawny smiled. 'Look at that,' she said to Lucy. 'Even the big children are tired.'

'I can hardly keep my eyes open,' said Holly.

'It's the sea air,' Mrs Trelawny said as she took Lucy's hand. 'You should have an early bed tonight.'

Holly watched as Mrs Trelawny and Lucy and Rags went out. The housekeeper was right. An early bed was exactly what she needed.

'Do you think your dad will mind us missing dinner?' she said.

Peter yawned. 'I couldn't eat a thing after that,' he said. 'Anyway Mr Allenbury and Dad are in the study. They'll be ages yet.'

Miranda grinned. 'Softies,' she said and then she yawned too.

'Look who's talking,' said Holly. She rose and stretched. 'I don't care if I am a softie,' she said. 'I'm going to read a couple of chapters of *The Secret of the China Pig* and then fall asleep.'

'I'm going to see if I can find one of those books about wreckers and smuggling in the library,' said Miranda.

'I'll come with you,' said Peter. 'I'd like to see if there are any books about seabirds.'

The library was huge. Bookcases lined the

walls, stretching right up to the ceiling. Leather chairs and small tables stood here and there. Facing the door was a large oak writing desk with a leather swivel chair behind it.

'How on earth are we going to find anything here?' said Peter. 'There must be thousands of books!'

Miranda gave a whoop of delight. 'I love those,' she said, making a dive for the swivel chair.

She planted herself in the chair and twirled it round.

'*Wheee*!' she said as she spun round.

'Miranda!' said Holly who'd followed the other two to the library. 'What if Mrs Trelawny sees you?'

Miranda let the chair stop twirling and came to rest facing the bookcase behind the desk.

'Look!' she said, jumping up. 'That's exactly what I'm looking for.'

She pulled a book down from one of the shelves.

'What is it?' said Peter. He was searching along a row of shelves.

'It's called *Stories of the Cornish Wreckers*,'

said Miranda, holding up the heavy book. 'Just what I wanted.'

And I've got a book about seabirds,' said Peter. He stretched up and took a book down. 'What a great idea – having your own library.'

'I wish we could have one,' said Holly. 'What would we have in it?'

'*Harriet the Spy* of course,' said Miranda as she and Peter walked towards her.

'We could have a video library as well,' said Peter. He switched off the library lights and the three of them trooped out into the hall.

Holly closed the library door. 'We could have videotapes of John Raven,' she said as they made their way upstairs.

Secret Agent John Raven was the star of *Spyglass*, the Mystery Kids' favourite television programme.

Holly yawned again. 'Even the most exciting episode of *Spyglass* wouldn't keep me awake tonight,' she said.

'Me neither,' said Peter. 'I'm whacked. See you in the morning.' And he turned into his own room.

Holly pushed open the door of the room she was sharing with Miranda.

'This is the most amazing house,' said Miranda following her.

'Mmm,' said Holly, starting to undress. 'I'm looking forward to exploring it.'

'I'll bet it's got a fascinating history,' Miranda said. 'I wonder if there are any stories about it in that book I got from the library.'

'The only story I'm interested in tonight is *The Secret of the China Pig*,' said Holly. But even *The Secret of the China Pig* couldn't keep Holly awake. Her eyes were already closing as Miranda climbed into bed with her book, still muttering about wreckers.

'Goodnight,' Holly said sleepily. And she yawned again as her eyes closed completely.

Holly woke up. The room was entirely dark. Not even a chink of light came through the thick curtains. For a moment, she lay there, puzzled. Then she looked at the luminous dial on her watch. It was after two o'clock. What had woken her?

She sat up. There had been something – some sound. Holly frowned, trying to remember. That was it. She had heard a dog bark. She lay back on her pillow. It was only Rags. Then she was sitting up again, wide awake. A great crash resounded through the room, shaking the window-panes.

'What's that?' said a sleepy voice from the other bed.

Holly got out of bed and made her way to the window. She pulled back the curtains. Outside, great drops of rain began to spatter the window and a flash of lightning lit up the whole sky.

'It's a storm,' Holly said to Miranda.

'Mmm,' said Miranda. 'For a minute I thought it was ghosts.'

Holly laughed, still looking out of the window. 'It's a wonder you didn't get nightmares reading that book about the wreckers,' she said.

Thunder crashed and lightning streaked the sky. The rain was falling in sheets now. It was so heavy Holly could hardly see the garden, just the shapes of branches blowing wildly in the wind.

Miranda switched on her bedside lamp and came to stand beside her. 'I *was* dreaming about wreckers,' she said, shivering.

She looked out at the sky. Lightning flashed and the trees below waved wildly. 'Cripes. You can just imagine wreckers out there on a night like this.' Miranda's eyes glowed. 'I can see them,' she said. 'Struggling through the wind down to the beach, lighting beacons to lure a ship on to the rocks and then . . .' She paused dramatically. 'Then the ship striking the rocks, the shouts of the sailors, the waves crashing over them and the wreckers waiting to steal the cargo.'

Holly looked at her. Miranda's eyes were tightly closed now. She was seeing the whole thing in her mind.

'You'll frighten yourself,' Holly warned.

Miranda opened her eyes and laughed loudly.

Holly grinned and let the curtain drop. Miranda's laugh would scare off dozens of wreckers.

'Something woke me up,' she said, dropping on to her bed.

Miranda came and perched beside her as another crash of thunder rattled the window.

'I'm not surprised,' she said. 'That would

wake the dead.' Her eyes sparkled. 'It probably did. Greystones is probably haunted by the ghosts of old wreckers and smugglers.' She curled her arms round her knees. 'I bet the house is full of secret passages and stuff!'

'No,' said Holly. 'I mean something else woke me up. I don't think it was the storm.'

Miranda shook her head. 'Headless corpses and pirates,' she said. 'They probably roam the house when there's a storm, wringing their hands and moaning about how sorry they are they did it.'

'Did what?' said Holly.

Miranda grinned. 'Wrecked the ships, stole the treasure, murdered the sailors.'

Holly laughed. 'You're impossible,' she said.

Miranda yawned. 'Oh, I'm tired,' she said. 'Imagining is hard work.'

She got up and crawled into her own bed, switching off her lamp. 'Goodnight,' she said sleepily.

Holly shook her head. How could Miranda just go to sleep with all that gruesome stuff in her head?

'I *did* hear something,' she said.

Miranda yawned again, her voice muffled. 'Probably Mrs Trelawny's piskies,' she said, her voice drifting away.

Holly lay down and stared into the darkness. Of course Rags would bark if he heard thunder. Lots of dogs were frightened of thunder. But something still bothered Holly. She lay awake for a long time. She couldn't sleep. What if there was a burglar in the house? She looked across at Miranda. She was fast asleep.

Quietly, Holly slipped out of bed and across to the bedroom door. She opened it. The house was completely dark.

She crept to the head of the stairs and looked down. A flash of lightning lit the hall below and in the momentary brightness Holly saw the library door standing open. She was sure she had closed it earlier. Maybe someone else had been in there. Or maybe somebody was in there now. It was worth investigating.

On silent bare feet Holly crept down the staircase. The old stairs creaked as she went. Around her, draughts blew and windows rattled with the sound of rain. Was that a noise in the library? Holly's heart began to beat faster. *Oh, why didn't I get my torch?*

She forced herself to cross the hall to the library door. A flash of lightning lit the room. There was nobody there. The wind whistled in the chimney and Holly shivered. She was certain she had heard a noise. She pressed down the light switch. Nothing. The storm must have cut the power.

Holly shivered again. She couldn't get rid of the feeling that something was wrong. The rain was stopping now, the thunder rolling away. The storm must be moving on. Suddenly the old house seemed very quiet. There was only the whisper of rain at the windows, the creak of old wooden floors and beams.

Was that a sound? Holly whirled round quickly and her heart leaped as she saw a dark shape hunched by the front door. Was Miranda right? Did the ghosts of ancient wreckers walk the house when there was a storm?

Then she almost laughed with relief. It was only a coatstand. She gave herself a shake. She was getting jumpy.

She turned and scampered upstairs to bed, not stopping until she was warm and safe under the duvet. Mysteries were OK. But ghosts – that was something else.

Lucy disappears

'That was quite a storm last night,' said Mr Hamilton.

Holly looked at him across the breakfast table. She had woken to a beautiful morning. The sky was washed a clear blue and the sun was already hot.

'What storm?' said Peter.

Mr Hamilton laughed. 'Peter, you would sleep through anything,' he said.

Peter grinned. 'I went to sleep straight away,' he said. 'I was so tired.'

Peter's words made Holly remember something. 'The downstairs lights wouldn't work,' she said. 'The storm must have cut the power.'

Mrs Trelawny put a dish of fluffy scrambled eggs on the table. 'They're all right now,' she said. 'But we often have a power cut when there's a storm.'

Mr Hamilton was looking at Holly. 'What were you doing downstairs?' he said.

Miranda speared a sausage from a dish on to her plate. 'Holly thought she heard something,' she said. 'She gave Holly a look. 'But I didn't know you went downstairs,' she said.

Holly concentrated on her bacon and eggs. She felt a bit silly when she remembered how frightened she had been. Imagine being scared by Miranda's stories of headless ghosts and pirates!

'I'm not surprised you heard *something* last night,' Mr Hamilton said.

Holly looked at him. 'Were you in the library last night?' she said.

Mr Hamilton looked puzzled. 'What a funny question,' he said. 'No. Mr Allenbury and I were in his study after dinner. And we both went up to bed after we'd finished our work.'

Mrs Trelawny was pouring a cup of coffee for Mr Hamilton. 'Is something wrong?' she said to Holly.

Holly shook her head. She was still feeling foolish. 'No, nothing,' she said.

Then she caught Peter's eye. He didn't believe her.

'Mrs Trelawny,' Miranda said. 'Are there any secret passageways in the house? I think there must be. I mean there must have been smuggling round here.'

Mrs Trelawny smiled and shook her head. 'I wouldn't know about that,' she said. 'I've got too much to do without looking for sliding panels and secret passages.'

'Don't take any notice of them,' Mr Hamilton said. 'These three are always on the lookout for mysteries.'

'And we find them, Dad,' said Peter, grinning. 'Or they find us.'

Mr Hamilton shook his head. 'Sometimes I wish they didn't,' he said.

Mrs Trelawny put her head on one side. 'Now you come to mention it . . .' she said. 'My mother worked here as a housemaid many years ago – long before she married. She talked about there being a secret passage somewhere in the house.'

'I told you so!' Miranda said, her eyes shining.

'Where?' Peter asked excitedly.

Mrs Trelawny shook her head. 'I don't think she ever knew,' she said. 'It was probably just a story.' She gave Miranda a look. 'Some people have a lot of imagination. You'll always find somebody making up stories about an old house like this.'

'Well, I wish somebody had woken me up last night,' Peter said. 'I love storms.'

Mrs Trelawny laughed. 'You should come to live in Cornwall,' she said. 'We get plenty of storms round here.'

'And wrecks,' said Miranda, ghoulishly.

The dining-room door opened and Mr Allenbury came in. He looked flustered.

'Your breakfast is ready, Mr Allenbury,' Mrs Trelawny said.

Mr Allenbury waved breakfast away. 'Sorry, Mrs Trelawny,' he said. 'I don't have time for breakfast this morning. I have to go to Exeter on urgent business.'

Mrs Trelawny looked surprised. 'Right away?' she asked. 'Surely you have time for a cup of coffee.'

'No!' Mr Allenbury said sharply. 'I've got to go.'

Holly looked up, surprised. Mr Allenbury's voice was quite curt. She and Miranda looked at each other and Miranda mouthed the word 'smuggler' at her.

'We'll look after Lucy,' said Peter. 'Can

we take her to the beach if we don't let her swim?'

Mr Allenbury's mouth set in a hard line. 'Lucy isn't here,' he said.

Mrs Trelawny gasped. 'Where is she?' she said.

Mr Allenbury turned away. 'I took her to Polperro first thing this morning,' he said. 'She'll be there for a few days. Jane phoned to ask if she could have Lucy to stay.'

'Jane?' said Holly before she could stop herself.

Mr Allenbury looked at Holly impatiently. 'Lucy's aunt, my sister,' he said. 'She lives in Polperro.'

'That's a pity,' said Mrs Trelawny. 'Lucy was looking forward to getting to know these three,' and she looked from Holly to Peter and Miranda. She looked thoughtful. 'Lucy has a dentist's appointment at the end of the week. I'll ring and let her aunt know.'

Mr Allenbury turned sharply to her. 'Don't do that, Mrs Trelawny,' he said.

Mrs Trelawny looked surprised. 'Why ever not?' she said. 'You're always so careful about her check-ups.'

Mr Allenbury ran a hand through his hair.

'Because Jane was thinking of taking Lucy on a trip,' he said. 'She wasn't sure how long she and Lucy would be away. But she'll make sure Lucy is back for her appointment. I told her about it.'

Mrs Trelawny shook her head. 'I don't see why she had to go so early,' she said. 'And with no breakfast.'

'I gave her some cereal,' Mr Allenbury said shortly. 'Don't interfere, Mrs Trelawny. I must go. And I have to see Jordan first.' He turned to Mr Hamilton. 'You'll find those books we were talking about in the library,' he said. And, with that, he was gone.

Mrs Trelawny stood looking after him with her mouth open. 'Well!' she said. 'I've never known Mr Allenbury talk to me like that before. And as for taking Lucy to Polperro this morning, I can hardly believe it. I didn't even know he was out of the house.'

Holly, Peter and Miranda looked at one another. Miranda's eyes were round with excitement.

Mr Hamilton got up from the table. 'It's a pity Mr Allenbury had to go,' he said. 'He and I were going to look at those books together. He seemed really keen to go over them with me.'

'What books?' said Peter, dragging his eyes away from Miranda. Miranda was nearly bursting with excitement.

'Just some old books about the house,' Mr Hamilton said. 'They have descriptions of the conservatory as it used to be. And I want to restore it to what it was like as much as possible.' He turned to Mrs Trelawny. 'Let me give you a hand taking these things out,' he said.

Mrs Trelawny still looked shaken. 'That's very good of you,' she said.

Holly, Peter and Miranda waited until Mrs Trelawny and Mr Hamilton had gone.

'What did I tell you?' Miranda said. 'I *knew* there was something funny going on.'

'What do you mean?' said Peter.

Miranda leaned across the table. 'Holly heard noises last night.'

'That was the storm,' Peter said.

Miranda ignored him. 'And then, this morning, Lucy disappears.'

Holly frowned. 'She's supposed to be in Polperro,' she said. 'With her aunt.'

Miranda shook her head. 'Maybe she is,'

she said. 'The important thing is she's out of the way.'

'Hang on,' said Peter. 'What are you suggesting? I mean it's Lucy's father you're talking about.'

Miranda narrowed her eyes. 'I think he's a smuggler. I think Holly *did* hear something last night.'

'I'm sure it wasn't just the storm,' Holly said. 'I thought at first it was Rags barking.'

'And that's another thing,' said Miranda. 'Where is Rags?'

'With Lucy,' said Peter. 'Rags goes everywhere with her.'

'Maybe,' said Miranda darkly. 'But it doesn't stop me thinking Mr Allenbury is up to something. Look how jumpy he was this morning.'

Peter nodded. 'That's true,' he said. 'He was quite different yesterday.'

'And why did he suddenly have to rush off to Exeter?' said Holly.

'And why is he going to see Jordan?' Miranda said.

Holly and Peter looked at her. 'OK, why?' said Peter.

Miranda narrowed her eyes. 'Because he's a smuggler,' she repeated. 'Because he and Jordan are in it together. Because he had to get Lucy out of the way.'

'But why?' said Holly.

Miranda's face was serious. 'Because something is going to happen very soon,' she said. 'Maybe tonight.'

Holly opened her mouth to argue but the door swung open and Mrs Trelawny came in with a tray. She still looked upset.

'Well,' she said, piling dishes on to the tray. 'All I can say is there's something funny going on. If Lucy had cereal this morning I'm a monkey's uncle.'

'What?' said Holly.

Mrs Trelawny turned to her. Her eyes were troubled.

'That child won't eat cereal unless she has a banana chopped up into it,' she said.

Holly frowned.

'And there was only one banana left in the bowl yesterday,' Mrs Trelawny went on.

'And?' said Holly.

'And it's still there,' Mrs Trelawny said.

53

'Wherever Lucy went, she didn't have cereal for breakfast before she left.'

Holly, Peter and Miranda looked at one another. There was no doubt about it. This was a real mystery.

5 Spying on Jordan

'So why lie about the cereal?' Miranda said.

Holly, Peter and Miranda were perched on the window seat in the girls' bedroom. They were half hidden by the curtains but they had a great view of the garden. Mr Allenbury and Jordan, the gardener, were deep in conversation at the far end of the lawn.

'Miranda's right,' said Peter. 'If he's lied about that then he could be up to anything.'

Holly frowned. 'But where is Lucy?' she said. 'Do you think she's really with her aunt?'

'And if she isn't, then where can she be?' said Miranda.

'I think you're right,' said Peter. 'I think Mr Allenbury just wanted her out of the way. I mean, he's her dad. She'll be OK wherever she is.'

Miranda bit her lip. 'I suppose he really *is* her dad,' she said.

'Don't be daft,' said Peter. 'Of course he is. She's not so young she doesn't know her own dad.'

'Maybe he's an imposter,' said Miranda. 'Maybe when her mum died in that car crash, her dad died too. She was only a baby. Maybe Mr Allenbury claimed he was her dad.' She sat up, eyes shining. 'Maybe he's her wicked uncle, her dad's twin brother and she's an heiress to a fortune and he wants to get hold of it.'

'Hang on,' said Peter. 'I thought he was a smuggler.'

Miranda looked stubborn. 'He could be both,' she said.

Holly shook her head. 'Honestly, Miranda,' she said. 'You're amazing. You nearly had me believing all that stuff about twin brothers for a minute.'

'It might be true,' said Miranda.

Holly looked at the two men on the lawn. 'I wish they weren't so far away,' she said. 'I wish we could see their faces.'

'Wait a minute,' said Peter. He leaped off the window seat and rushed out of the room.

'I'm going to learn to lip-read,' Miranda said. 'All spies should be able to lip-read.'

'We can't even see their lips,' said Holly.

'We can now,' said Peter, coming back into the room. He waved his binoculars at them, then positioned himself in front of the window.

'What's going on?' said Miranda, jumping up and down.

'Wow!' said Peter. 'Jordan looks angry and Mr Allenbury's face is as white as a sheet.'

'Something's gone wrong with their plans,' Holly said. 'That's why Mr Allenbury has to go to Exeter. There must be a hitch and Jordan's angry.'

Suddenly the two men drew apart. Mr Allenbury turned and strode towards the house.

'Get down,' said Peter. 'He might look up and see us.'

The three of them ducked, chins resting on the window seat.

'But we won't see where they're going,' Miranda wailed.

Peter looked at her. 'Do you want them to know we're suspicious?' he said.

Miranda shook her head. 'Sometimes I

57

wish we could make ourselves invisible,' she said. 'Spying would be so much easier.'

There was the sound of a car engine and wheels spurted on the gravel drive below the window.

'That's Mr Allenbury going away,' Holly said.

But Peter was looking at Miranda. 'Miranda, you're brilliant,' he said.

Miranda lifted her eyebrows. 'Well, I know that,' she said. Then she looked suspicious. 'But why exactly?'

Peter was on his feet, the binoculars in his hands.

'We can't follow Mr Allenbury,' he said. 'But we can follow Jordan – and spy on him.'

'He'll yell at us and chase us if he sees us spying on him,' Holly said.

'He won't see us,' said Peter. 'We'll be invisible.'

'What?' said Miranda.

Peter waved the binoculars and grinned. 'Bird-watching,' he said. 'We take the binoculars and the camera and a notebook – and go bird-watching. There's nothing suspicious about that.'

'And all the time we'll be Jordan-watching,' Miranda said.

Holly peered out of the window. 'There's just one drawback,' she said.

'What's that?' said Peter.

Holly turned to him. 'Jordan has disappeared,' she said.

'Oh, no,' said Miranda. 'You don't think he's gone off with Mr Allenbury?'

Peter shook his head. 'They started off in opposite directions,' he said. He grinned at them. 'Come on, get the camera and a notebook. We're going Jordan-watching.'

'If we can find him,' Miranda said gloomily.

'Of course we can,' said Holly. 'Let's get on his trail. They don't call us the Mystery Kids for nothing. And I've got an idea where he might be.'

'There he is!' Peter said in a whisper.

Holly and Miranda crouched down beside him under the trees.

'Where?' said Miranda.

'Just coming out of the summer-house,' Peter said.

'That summer-house again,' said Holly. 'There's something going on there.'

59

Miranda nodded. 'That's probably where they're going to stash the stuff.'

'What stuff?' said Peter.

'The stuff they're smuggling,' Miranda said impatiently. 'Look, he's coming this way.'

Holly, Peter and Miranda melted back into the trees as Jordan made his way across the clearing.

'What do we do now?' said Miranda.

'Keep following him,' said Peter. 'But silently.'

It wasn't easy avoiding crackly twigs and broken branches, but they managed to trail Jordan back towards the steps at the bottom of the lawns without being seen or heard.

'Look,' said Peter. 'He's taking the cliff path.'

'The one he warned us not to take,' said Peter.

'Let's wait till he's out of sight and go back and have a look in the summer-house,' Holly said.

'Good idea,' said Peter. 'We might get a clue to what they're up to. He might have been leaving something in there.'

The Mystery Kids waited breathlessly until

Jordan turned a corner in the path. Then they sprinted for the summer-house.

'Ugh!' said Holly, pulling open the door. 'It's as dusty as ever.'

Peter was raking round the room, lifting cushions, looking under the chairs. 'There's nothing that wasn't here before,' he said.

'So what was Jordan doing in here?' Miranda said.

Holly shrugged. 'Checking it out?' she said. 'Making sure it was OK for stashing whatever they're smuggling.'

Miranda looked doubtful. 'I suppose so,' she said.

'OK,' said Peter. 'Let's not waste any more time here. Let's get after Jordan.'

'I'm with you,' said Holly. 'This place is so smelly. It's horrible.'

'I still think it would make a great head-quarters,' said Miranda as they came out into the wood.

'No time for that now,' said Peter. 'Come on. We don't want Jordan to give us the slip again.'

They pelted back towards the cliff path.

'Try not to make too much noise,' Holly warned.

61

The path was straight for a while, then it took a sharp bend and plunged downwards.

'*Aaah*!' yelled Miranda as her feet skidded on the sandy soil.

'Watch out,' said Peter, grabbing her.

Holly came round the bend and stopped. 'Cripes!' she said. 'Look at that!'

On their left, the ground sloped sharply away and dropped towards high cliffs.

'Oh, no,' said Peter, still holding on to Miranda.

'What?' said Holly.

Peter didn't answer. He didn't have to.

'Get out of there, you kids,' Jordan yelled.

He was standing below them on the cliff path, his face red and angry. 'Go on, get out of here. I told you before not to come down here. It's dangerous.'

'So much for following him,' Miranda said glumly as the three of them turned back up the path.

But Holly was looking over to the right now, where the cliff rose even higher, curving round the bay.

'Look,' she said, pointing to a clump of grass on the edge of the cliff. 'I bet you'd get a great view to the bottom of the path from up there. The cliff curves round.'

Peter looked back down the path. 'And Jordan must be going down there,' he said. 'You can just see the end of the path. There's no other way to go.'

'Right,' said Miranda. 'What are we waiting for? Let's get going.'

She turned back and looked down the path. Jordan was still standing there. 'Sorry,' she called sweetly. 'We took the wrong turning.'

Jordan didn't say anything but he stood watching them until they were out of sight.

'Phew!' said Holly as she slumped down behind the clump of grass. 'I didn't realise it would be such a stiff climb.'

'But what a view,' Peter said. 'Look, you can see where the cliff path comes out.'

Miranda shaded her eyes from the sun and peered through the strands of grass. 'It's a little bay,' she said. 'But where's Jordan?'

Holly squinted against the sun. 'He can't have disappeared,' she said. 'There's nowhere else to go. Look, the bay is enclosed on both sides.'

Peter put the binoculars to his eyes. 'There are sheer cliffs coming right down either side,' he said. 'The only way out is by the cliff path.'

'He didn't come back up,' Miranda said. 'We would have seen him.'

'Hang on,' said Holly. 'What's that? Peter, look through your binoculars on the far side of the bay. I thought I saw something moving.'

Peter adjusted the binoculars. 'There *is* something,' he said. 'It's white and there's metal on it, but I can't tell what it is.' He paused. 'It's moving,' he said.

'Sounds mysterious,' said Miranda. 'Let me see.'

'Wait a minute,' said Peter. 'There's Jordan!'

Holly strained her eyes to see. She could make out a dark shape against the cliff face. 'Where did he come from?' she said.

Peter lowered the binoculars and turned to her. 'You aren't going to believe this,' he said. 'But it looked as if he walked straight out of the rock.'

Holly looked at Peter, amazed.

'That's impossible,' she said.

'Oh, no,' said Miranda. 'There's another

man down there and he's seen us. Quick, Peter, give me the binoculars!'

She grabbed the binoculars out of Peter's hands and looked through them out to sea. 'Take a picture of Holly and me,' she said.

Holly threw Peter the camera and he pretended to take a picture.

'What I really want is a picture of those two,' he said. 'Not that it'll be much good from this distance without a telephoto lens. Move over a bit.'

'What are they doing?' said Holly. She and Miranda had their backs to the bay.

Peter shifted the camera slightly and started snapping away furiously. 'They've seen us,' he said. 'But I think it's OK. They've started up the cliff path.'

'Do you think they're coming to get us?' said Holly.

'What can they do?' said Peter. 'Throw us into the sea? Shove us off the cliff?'

Holly heard Jordan's voice again. 'We don't want any accidents, do we?' She shivered. 'Don't say things like that, Peter,' she said.

'What are we going to do?' said Miranda.

'Stay here,' said Holly. 'Till we're sure they've gone.'

'And then we're going to investigate,' said Peter. 'I don't believe anybody can walk straight out of a cliff. There's something really odd happening down there.'

'Meanwhile,' said Holly, 'we've got to look as if we really are studying seabirds.'

'That's OK by me,' said Peter. 'Bird-watching is really interesting.'

Holly and Miranda looked at each other. Peter liked bird-watching. He also liked collecting car registration numbers. Holly and Miranda couldn't see the point in any of it.

'Still,' said Holly to Miranda. 'Bird-watching makes a pretty good excuse for going round with binoculars.'

Miranda giggled. 'What do you get if you run over a bird with a lawn-mower?' she said.

Holly groaned. 'Go on, tell me,' she said.

'Shredded tweet!' Miranda shrieked with laughter.

'Miranda,' Peter said. 'You nearly gave that herring gull a heart attack. You've got to be quiet when you're bird-watching.'

'Well, that's one hobby Miranda won't be taking up,' said Holly.

'I'm not interested in mouldy old birds,' said Miranda. 'It's smugglers I'm after.'

66

But by the time Jordan and his friend had climbed back up the cliff path, Miranda was totally absorbed in bird-watching. Holly and Peter had to drag her away.

'Nobody told me bird-watching was so absorbing,' she said as they slithered down the cliff path. 'And it's terrific practice for spying.'

Peter grinned. 'So is collecting car registration numbers,' he said.

Miranda made a face at him.

'Here's the bay,' said Holly, skidding down the last bit of the path. She looked round. 'It's OK. It's empty.'

'I keep thinking they're going to jump out at us,' Miranda said nervously as they explored the bay.

'We saw them go into the woods,' Peter said. 'I just wish I knew who that other man was.'

'You don't think they saw you taking photographs?' Holly said.

Peter frowned. 'I hope they thought I was taking photos of you two,' he said.

'It's just a bay,' Holly said looking round. 'Nothing mysterious.'

'There must be *something*,' said Miranda.

'And where is that white thing I saw?' said Peter.

Miranda was clambering over rocks, peering round outcrops of the cliff.

'Hey!' she yelled. 'Over here. Look what I've found.'

Peter and Holly scrambled after her. The outcrop of cliff hid a deep inlet. The water ran under the cliff for a little way. And there, rocking at anchor, was a white motor-boat. Round the inlet was a narrow ledge, broad enough to walk on.

'That's what I saw,' said Peter, looking at the motor-boat. 'And this is where they came from. No wonder it looked as if they walked straight out of the solid rock. You'd never see right into this inlet from the cliff top.'

'You don't even see it from the bay,' Holly said.

Peter was clambering round the far side of the outcrop.

'What are you doing?' Miranda said.

Peter looked back at her and grinned. 'Investigating, of course,' he said. 'I want to see what they've got in that boat.'

'Diamonds!' guessed Miranda. 'Or gold bars.'

Peter's grin got wider. 'Or maybe diving equipment,' he said. Then he leaped lightly from the outcrop on to the ledge.

'Be careful,' said Holly as Peter made his way along the ledge. Drifted sand had piled up on it.

Holly watched as Peter inched his way along. Then he bent his knees and jumped into the boat. It rocked violently and waves rippled out of the cave, splashing the girls.

'*Hoi!*' Miranda yelled. 'I'm soaked.'

But Peter was bent double, searching the boat. He looked up.

'I don't know what those two are up to,' he said. 'But they're definitely up to something.'

'What have you found?' said Miranda.

Peter looked at the girls. 'This boat is all ready to go,' he said. 'There's food and fuel and all sorts of stuff. I reckon it's ready for a getaway.'

'A getaway,' Miranda breathed.

'You mean they really *are* smugglers?' said Holly.

Peter looked serious. 'It certainly looks like it.' He bent down and started looking at the boat. His face took on a thoughtful look.

Holly and Miranda looked at each other.

'What did I tell you?' Miranda said.

Holly started to speak, then she clutched Miranda's arm.

'What was that?' she said.

'What?' said Miranda.

The sound came again. A high-pitched sound, like a scream. It came from the bay on the other side of the outcrop.

'There's somebody else here,' said Holly. 'There's someone in the bay.'

6 A strange appearance

'Who do you think it is?' whispered Miranda nervously.

Holly swallowed. 'I hope it isn't Jordan,' she said. 'Or his friend.'

'Should we go and investigate?' Miranda said.

Holly looked into the cave mouth. Peter was crouched down in the boat. All his attention was on something he was examining. She bit her lip. If she raised her voice above a whisper, whoever was on the other side of the rock outcrop might hear her. And if it was Jordan or his accomplice, she certainly didn't want them to hear her.

The sound came again. Then there was a scrabbling noise.

'You don't think someone has fallen over the cliff, do you?' said Miranda.

Holly stared at her. 'It couldn't be Lucy,

71

could it?' she said. 'I mean, if you're right and she isn't in Polperro . . .' Her voice trailed away.

'I think we ought to investigate,' Miranda said.

Holly nodded. 'Let's keep really quiet though,' she said. 'In case it's Jordan.'

Miranda nodded.

Holly started off round the outcrop, keeping close to the cliff wall.

'What can you see?' Miranda whispered in her ear.

Holly poked her head round the outcrop. The bay was empty – at least what she could see of it was empty.

'Nothing,' she whispered back.

Miranda gave her a little push. 'Go on,' she said.

Holly inched round the outcrop. Now she could see the whole bay. There was nobody there. Breathless with relief, she jumped down on to the sand. 'There's no one here,' she said.

Miranda followed her, her face puzzled. 'But there must be. We heard them.'

Then she stopped. The sound came again. 'It's coming from over there,' said Holly, pointing to a rock-fall at the bottom of the cliff.

'You go first,' said Miranda.

Holly grabbed her. 'Not on your life,' she said. 'We go together.'

Cautiously, the girls approached the fallen rocks. Several large lumps of the cliff had tumbled down on to the beach. Holly could tell they had been there a long time; they were slippery with seaweed. She stretched out a hand to steady herself as she made her way across the rocks. She looked down.

'Look, Miranda!' she cried.

Miranda slid down beside her.

'It's Rags,' she said. 'Poor little thing. He might be hurt.'

Holly looked up. 'He can't have fallen down here,' she said. 'The cliff-face is sheer. He'd never have survived it.'

'What's that?' said Miranda pointing to a shallow opening in the cliff-face just a metre or two from the rock-fall.

Holly looked. 'He could have scrambled down from there,' she said. 'But how did he get there in the first place?'

Miranda shrugged. 'I don't know,' she said.

Rags opened his eyes and looked up at them. He whimpered again and gave a yelp, then his paws scrabbled uselessly at the slippery rocks.

'Anyway, who cares how he got here?' said Miranda. 'Let's get him out of there.'

Carefully the girls eased and edged the little dog out of the cleft in the rocks. Holly gathered him into her arms. He was cold and shivering and he yipped sharply as she clutched him. Her fingers touched something warm and moist.

'He's bleeding,' she said. 'There's a cut on his side.'

Miranda scrambled across the rocks and made for the outcrop just as Peter appeared.

'What's going on?' he called.

'Quick!' Miranda yelled. 'We've found Rags. And he's hurt. We'd better get him up to the house as soon as possible.'

Peter looked up sharply. 'Rags?' he said.

'Yes,' said Miranda impatiently as Holly leaped down from the rocks on to the sand. 'Rags, Lucy's little terrier.'

Peter shook his hair out of his eyes. 'I know who Rags is,' he said.

'So what's wrong?' said Holly, looking at

Peter. He was looking really worried. Rags shivered in her arms. They had to get him back home soon.

'Only this,' said Peter. 'If Rags is here, where is Lucy? You know the two of them are never apart.'

Holly felt her breath catch. Her hands tightened on Rags and he yelped.

'Sorry, Rags,' she said and bent to rub her nose on his head. Then she looked from Peter to Miranda.

'I guess we'd better start looking for her,' Miranda said.

'She isn't in the bay,' said Peter after they'd searched for ten minutes. 'It's so tiny; we'd have seen her.'

The same thought had occurred to all of them. If Rags had fallen on to the rocks, Lucy could have done the same. But they had looked behind every rock, every outcrop. Lucy wasn't anywhere on the beach.

Nobody said anything about the tides. Holly didn't want to think about what might have happened to Lucy if she had been with Rags. If she had fallen and the tide had come in, she could have been swept out to sea.

'But Lucy's in Polperro,' she said for the umpteenth time.

Peter and Miranda looked at her. They would all have liked to believe that.

'Without Rags?' said Peter.

'Mr Allenbury didn't say anything about taking Rags to Polperro,' Miranda said.

Holly thought. 'Maybe he left Rags behind. Maybe Rags tried to follow them and came down here and . . .' She stopped. And what?

'That'll be it,' Peter said briskly. 'Rags got left behind and he tried to follow them and got trapped down here.'

Holly, Peter and Miranda looked at one another. Even if Rags *had* followed Lucy and Mr Allenbury, what had they been doing down here in the first place? But that had to be the explanation – hadn't it?

'Let's get Rags back to the house,' said Peter. 'He needs looking after.'

'I think we should talk to your dad, Peter,' said Holly.

'And say what? That we think Mr Allenbury is a smuggler.' Peter was right; if they wanted Mr Hamilton to believe them, they needed proof.

It wasn't easy climbing the cliff path with

the terrier in her arms but Holly managed it. She was glad when they reached the house.

'Who's there?' Mrs Trelawny called as they went in by the front door.

The housekeeper came out of the library, a duster in her hand.

'It's only us,' said Peter.

Mrs Trelawny looked relieved. 'I thought it was Jordan again,' she said. 'He was in the house earlier. I don't like him hanging round the house.'

Holly looked at the housekeeper. 'Why not, Mrs Trelawny?' she said.

Mrs Trelawny pursed her lips. 'Because I don't like him,' she said shortly. Then she looked at Rags. 'Where on earth did you find Rags?' she said. 'I didn't know he was here. I thought he'd gone with Lucy.'

Holly, Peter and Miranda looked at one another.

'We thought so too,' said Peter.

'Rags is hurt,' said Miranda.

Mrs Trelawny gave them a sharp look. 'Bring him into the kitchen and tell me what's happened,' she said.

Holly, Peter and Miranda explained as they went.

'But what was he doing down on the beach?' Mrs Trelawny said as they carried the bedraggled little bundle into the kitchen.

'We don't know,' said Miranda. 'But we'd like to find out.'

Mrs Trelawny fussed and tutted over Rags as Holly bathed the cut on his side. It had already stopped bleeding but there was still a tender patch. Mrs Trelawny brought a warm blanket to wrap round him and a dish of milk and some dog biscuits. The little terrier was clearly very hungry. He finished every last scrap.

Soon he was sitting up, shaking himself free of the blanket. But he was clearly unhappy. He kept running to and fro.

'Tut, tut,' said Mrs Trelawny. 'He's looking for Lucy.' She shook her head. 'Well, she's in Polperro,' she said to the little dog. 'But I don't suppose you'll be satisfied until you've searched the whole house, will you, Rags?'

Rags barked up at her, his tail wagging at the mention of Lucy's name.

Mrs Trelawny opened the kitchen door and the little terrier shot through. Holly saw him disappear in the direction of the hall.

78

'He doesn't seem too badly hurt,' said Peter.

'No,' said Holly. 'But he's going to be very disappointed when he doesn't find Lucy.'

'When is Lucy coming back?' Miranda said to Mrs Trelawny.

Mrs Trelawny shook her head. 'I don't know,' she said. 'But Mr Allenbury will be back tonight. He'll be able to tell you.'

Holly looked at Miranda. Mrs Trelawny clearly had no doubts about where Lucy was.

'And you three had better give yourselves a wash,' she said. 'Lunch will be ready in no time at all.'

Holly, Peter and Miranda looked at one another. Mrs Trelawny was right. They were covered in sand and bits of seaweed from their scramble round the rocks.

'At least Rags is all right now,' said Holly as the three of them trailed upstairs to wash.

Miranda and Peter nodded but none of them felt happy. There was something very odd going on. And they had no idea what it was.

A hidden lever

'I could do with a bit of help this afternoon,' said Mr Hamilton at lunch.

The Mystery Kids looked at one another. They had planned to spend the afternoon tracking Jordan and trying to find out who his mysterious friend was.

'What kind of help?' said Peter.

Mr Hamilton smiled. 'Research,' he said. 'There's a box of old photographs I'd like you to go through.'

'Of the house?' said Miranda, interested.

Mr Hamilton nodded. 'I want all the ones of the conservatory gathered together. I'm working my way through a mass of papers from years back, trying to find references to the conservatory. It was built by a very important architect and I want to get this restoration just right.' He looked at them. 'I know it'll take up your time,' he said.

'But Professor Crawford, the architect's great-grandson, lives nearby. I've arranged to go and have dinner with him tonight. So I want all the information I can get before then.'

Holly looked at Mr Hamilton. If it wasn't for him they wouldn't be here in the first place. They could hardly refuse to help him. 'Of course we'll help you, Mr Hamilton,' she said.

'It'll be good fun looking at old pictures of the house,' Miranda said.

'You never know what we might find,' said Peter.

'Good for you,' said Mr Hamilton.

'Here's another one,' said Holly as they sat surrounded by boxes of old photographs. They had brought the boxes into the library. She looked at the picture of the conservatory. 'It looks like a gingerbread house,' she said. 'Look at all those curly twirly bits.'

Peter laughed. 'Don't let my father hear you call them "curly twirly bits" or he'll give you a half-hour lecture about what they're really called.'

'I thought I might find some pictures of pirates and smugglers,' Miranda said.

'But all the people in these pictures look respectable.'

Holly and Peter laughed. 'Keep looking,' said Peter.

They were sitting at the library window. They had a good view of the lawn from there.

'At least we don't have to worry about keeping track of Jordan,' said Holly.

Peter looked across the lawn to where the gardener had been trimming a big yew hedge all afternoon. 'We couldn't have a better excuse for sitting here watching him,' he said.

The gardener looked over towards them and scowled.

'He doesn't look very happy,' said Miranda. She paused. 'I don't suppose he had anything to do with what happened to Rags.'

Holly looked at Jordan. 'I wouldn't be surprised if he did,' she said.

'Where *is* Rags?' said Peter.

Holly shrugged. 'I haven't seen him since before lunch. Mrs Trelawny thinks he'll be up in Lucy's room moping.'

'Poor little thing,' said Miranda. She looked up as the library door opened. 'Here's your dad, Peter.'

Mr Hamilton looked at the pile of photographs.

'You've done well,' he said, smiling. 'I really appreciate you giving up a whole afternoon. I think you deserve a treat. How would you like to come out to dinner with Professor Crawford and me?'

Peter screwed up his eyes. 'Would we have to get dressed up?' he said.

Mr Hamilton looked at the three of them in shorts and T-shirts.

'Well . . .' he said.

'We would, wouldn't we?' said Peter.

'All right,' said Mr Hamilton. 'Maybe it isn't a good idea. Tell you what. I'll take you out for lunch tomorrow instead. You can wear what you like and eat what you like.'

'You're on,' said Peter, grinning.

'We'd only get in the way tonight,' said Miranda. 'I mean you want to talk about this conservatory and all that.'

'And that would be boring,' said Mr Hamilton, laughing.

'Not boring,' Miranda said, thinking quickly. 'Just not very interesting.'

Mr Hamilton gathered up the photographs. 'I'll just go through these and then I'm off,' he said. 'Don't get up to any mischief tonight.'

'As if we would,' said Holly.

Mr Hamilton laughed again as he left the room.

Peter gazed out of the window. 'How about a swim before dinner?' he said.

'Good idea,' said Holly. 'And then we have to have a Mystery Kids meeting.

Miranda nodded. 'We've got to assemble all our clues,' she said. 'Try and figure out what's going on here.'

'After dinner,' Peter said. 'I think better after I've eaten.'

You eat all the time,' said Miranda.

'I do not,' said Peter.

'Come on, you two,' Holly said. 'Or it'll be too late to go for a swim.'

'Mrs Trelawny is a really great cook,' Peter said later as the three of them made their way upstairs after dinner.

Miranda nodded. Then she looked down into the hall where the shadows were beginning to draw in. She shivered. 'This house is spooky,' she said.

'I thought you liked it,' Holly said.

Miranda nodded. 'I do, but I wouldn't like to be all alone here.'

Peter twisted his face into a horrible mask and bounded on to the landing, crouching there.

'I'm Pirate Pete, come to haunt you,' he said.

Holly chuckled.

'Why didn't the ghost go to the disco?' said Miranda.

Holly looked accusingly at Peter. 'Now see what you've done,' she said.

Peter groaned and sat up. 'OK, tell us,' he said to Miranda.

'Because he hadn't any body to go with,' Miranda said and gave a hoot of laughter.

Peter clutched his ears. 'And that would scare away any self-respecting ghost,' he said.

Holly stepped over Peter and opened the door of his room.

'Let's get to work,' she said as the other two followed her. 'Where's your notebook, Peter?'

Peter went to his bedside table. 'Oh, no.' He bent and picked something up off the floor. 'My camera,' he said. 'It must have fallen off the table and the back has come loose. The film's exposed.'

'Now we don't have those pictures of Jordan and his friend,' said Holly.

'Or the boat,' said Peter.

Miranda narrowed her eyes. 'Maybe it didn't fall,' she said.

Holly turned to her. 'What do you mean?'

Miranda gave her a look. 'Mrs Trelawny was complaining about Jordan being in the house.'

'You mean maybe *he* did this?' said Peter.

'And made it look like an accident,' said Miranda.

Holly nodded. 'That's the first thing that goes in the notebook,' she said.

The three of them perched on Peter's bed.

'Right,' said Holly. 'What else?'

Miranda pursed up her mouth.

'First,' she said. 'Is Lucy really in Polperro?'

'Is Mr Allenbury really her dad?' said Peter.

Holly looked at him. 'You don't really believe that stuff about twin brothers,' she said.

Peter looked thoughtful. 'Maybe not,' he said. 'But Mr Allenbury is definitely suspicious.'

'What is Mr Allenbury up to?' Holly said, writing it down.

'Smuggling,' said Miranda.

'Why is he always talking to Jordan?' said Peter.

'He's the gardener,' Holly said.

'Or they're in this smuggling business together,' Peter said.

'Why does Jordan want us to keep away from the summer-house?' Miranda said.

'And the beach?' said Holly.

'We know that,' said Peter. 'He wants to keep that boat hidden.'

'That still leaves the summer-house,' said Holly.

'The summer-house could be a hideout – or a place to stash the stuff they're smuggling,' said Miranda.

'And who is the other guy that's with him?' said Miranda.

Holly was scribbling furiously. 'We've got an awful lot of questions and no answers,' she said. 'Or at least, no definite answers. Just a lot of ideas.'

'What we need are some hard facts,' said Miranda. 'All we've got at the moment are suspicions.'

Peter nodded. 'And here's another question. How did Rags get down on the beach?'

'And why isn't he with Lucy?' added Miranda.

Holly sat up. 'Poor Rags,' she said. 'I'd forgotten about him. I wonder where he is.'

'In Lucy's room probably,' Miranda said. 'But I think we ought to go and look. He must be miserable.'

'OK,' said Peter. 'I'll go.'

He was back within a minute. 'He isn't there,' he said.

Holly and Miranda looked worried.

'Then where is he?' Miranda said. 'Mrs Trelawny hadn't seen him.'

'We'd better search for him,' Holly said.

Peter nodded and picked up his torch.

'What's that for?' said Miranda.

Peter shrugged. 'Dogs are funny,' he said. 'If they're really miserable they creep away and hide in dark corners.'

Miranda jumped up. 'If we're looking in dark corners in this house, I'm going to get Holly's torch too,' she said.

'And I'll get some dog biscuits from Mrs Trelawny,' Peter said. 'That'll tempt him out of hiding.'

But they didn't find Rags in a dark corner. They found him in the library.

'There he is,' said Miranda as the three of them came into the library.

She pointed at the small furry bundle huddled at the foot of one of the bookcases. Holly walked softly towards Rags. She didn't want to alarm him.

'We've looked everywhere for you,' she said gently.

The little dog looked up at her pitifully. He was crouched against the bottom of the bookcase, whining and scrabbling at it.

'Come on, Rags,' said Peter, going to pick him up.

But the terrier growled deep in his throat.

'Maybe he's scared of you,' said Holly.

'Here you are, Rags,' said Peter, bringing out the dog biscuits. 'Come and get them.'

But Rags ignored the biscuits and huddled closer to the bookcase.

'Poor thing,' said Miranda. 'He's still terrified.'

She looked at the bookcase. 'Oh, look,' she said. 'There's another book on wreckers.'

She reached up and took the book off the

shelf. At that moment Rags jumped up and started pawing at the shelves.

'What is it, Rags?' Holly said.

Miranda let go of the book and it fell sideways along the shelf. There was a click and a whirr and the bookcase moved slightly.

Rags jumped up, barking furiously, sniffing at the bookcase.

'Look,' said Miranda. 'There's a lever in here behind these books.'

'What kind of lever?' said Holly. 'Why should there be a lever in a bookcase?'

Miranda licked her lips. 'I don't know,' she said. 'But there's only one way to find out.' She pressed down the lever.

Slowly one side of the bookcase slid towards them. It was on hinges, like a door. And as it opened Holly found herself looking into a dark passageway.

'It's a secret passage,' she said. 'I don't believe it!'

Rags dived through the opening and stood there, barking at them. Then he ran a little way in and back again.

'What is it, boy?' said Peter. He looked at the girls. 'I think he wants us to follow him.'

Holly was staring at the floor behind the bookcase. 'Look!' she managed to say at last.

There, lying on the floor, was one of Lucy's new hair ribbons.

Holly, Peter and Miranda looked at the bright blue ribbon and then at one another.

Holly stepped forward and picked up the ribbon. It seemed to bring Lucy very close.

'You don't think she could be in there, do you?' Miranda said.

Holly swallowed. There was a lump in her throat. The thought of the little girl in that dark place was awful.

'She can't be,' said Peter. 'How would she get in?'

'Maybe she accidentally pushed the lever,' Miranda said.

Holly looked at the lever and shook her head. 'It's too high up. She wouldn't be able to reach it.'

'Maybe it was open already,' said Peter.

'And she went inside to explore,' said Miranda.

'And the door shut behind her,' said Peter.

92

'But why would it be open?' Holly said.

Miranda frowned. 'The smugglers,' she said. 'Maybe it's their secret hiding-place.'

But Holly shook her head again. 'Even if it is,' she said, 'why would Mr Allenbury say she's in Polperro?'

'Unless he knew she was in there,' said Peter.

The three looked at one another.

'He wouldn't do that,' said Holly. 'Not to his own daughter.'

There was the sound of wheels on gravel. The light of powerful headlights flooded the room for a moment then swept by.

Peter whirled round but Holly was at the window before him. 'It's Mr Allenbury,' she said.

'What are we going to do?' said Miranda.

Peter took a deep breath. Rags was standing inside the entrance to the secret passage, barking.

'I think this settles it,' he said, looking at Lucy's hair ribbon clutched in Holly's hand. 'Even if Lucy isn't in there now, she must have been there sometime recently. I mean if Lucy is in Polperro, what's her hair ribbon doing here?'

'And I thought I heard a noise from the library last night,' said Holly.

Miranda's eyes were troubled. 'There's something very wrong here,' she said.

'Rags!' Holly shouted.

But Rags had got tired of waiting for them. He had turned and was hurtling down the passageway into the darkness beyond.

In the passageway

They heard the sound of the front door slam.

'It's Mr Allenbury,' said Miranda. 'What if he comes into the library? What if he finds us here?'

Peter dragged on the bookcase and swung it all the way open.

'He won't find us in here,' he said, snapping on his torch. 'Come on.' And he stepped into the secret passageway.

Holly and Miranda were right behind him.

'Where's Rags?' said Miranda.

Holly shrugged. 'He took off down the passageway. We'll just have to follow it and see if we can find him.'

'Quick,' said Peter. 'Close the entrance. Mr Allenbury might come into the library.'

Holly swung the heavy bookcase back towards her until it clicked. Darkness closed round them.

'It's all right,' said Miranda behind her. 'I've got your torch.'

Miranda flicked on the torch and held it under her chin. It made her face look monstrous.

'Don't do that,' said Holly, smiling in spite of herself. 'If Lucy is in here somewhere, you'll frighten her to death.'

'This place is enough to frighten anybody,' Miranda said, shining her torch on the walls.

'It looks really ancient,' said Holly. 'I don't think it's been used in years.'

Peter looked round. 'Ugh!' he said. 'Cobwebs! Do you think there are spiders in here?'

Peter hated spiders.

'The Mystery Kids are a match for anything, spiders included,' Miranda said.

'Of course we are,' said Holly. She gave Miranda a little push forward. 'Shine the torch on the floor so that we can see where we're walking.'

Miranda turned the torch beam downwards. The light helped, but Holly didn't say what was in her mind. The click as the bookcase slid into place had sounded final.

Holly just hoped they would be able to get out of the secret passage again.

Holly peered into the darkness beyond Miranda. She could see a faint glow from Peter's torch. She clutched little Lucy's hair ribbon in her hand. What would they find at the end of the passage?

The passage stretched in front of them. Their torch beams lit up rough walls and a stone-flagged floor. It was cold. Then the passage twisted to the right and began to run downwards. It seemed to go on for a long way.

'Where do you think it leads?' said Miranda nervously. She turned to Holly, her face glowing eerily in the torchlight.

Holly shook her head. 'I don't know,' she said.

'What if we never get out?' said Miranda.

'We'll get out,' said Holly with more confidence than she felt.

'There's a light down there,' Peter said. He turned to them. 'Don't make a noise,' he said.

Holly's heart began to pound. Had they discovered the smugglers' den? Were Jordan and his accomplice waiting for them there?

'I'm trying to work out which direction the passage is going in,' Holly said softly.

'The library faces the lawns,' Miranda whispered.

'And the bookcase was on the wall facing the door,' said Peter.

'But it twisted to the right,' said Miranda. 'That means the passageway runs towards the sea.'

'It must lead to the beach,' Holly said.

Miranda's eyes lit up. 'It's an old smugglers' route,' she whispered.

'Shh,' said Peter. 'Look!'

The girls looked where he was pointing. The passage turned to the right ahead of them. They could see the faint glow of a light. Then Holly jumped as a sudden noise shattered the silence. It echoed down the stone passageway, bouncing off the walls, filling the narrow space with echoes. Holly felt the hairs rise on the back of her neck.

'What on earth is that?' said Miranda, clutching Holly's arm.

Peter stood completely still for a moment, then he flattened himself against the wall.

'Get back against the wall and don't move,' he said to the girls. 'It's coming this way. And switch off your torch, Miranda.'

There was a double click as Peter and Miranda switched off the torches. Darkness enveloped them as they pressed themselves into the wall. Holly felt the breath stop in her throat as the unearthly sound filled the passageway. The rough stone of the passage wall was cold against her back. Then she heard a soft scuttling sound and something furry brushed against her ankle. She opened her mouth to scream.

'*Aaaaah!*' screeched Miranda before Holly could draw breath. 'Something horrible just brushed my leg.'

Peter switched on his torch and Holly heard him gasp.

Holly took a deep breath and looked down.

'Rags!' she said.

Miranda let out a whoop of relief.

'Of all the daft dogs,' she said, bending down and giving Rags a cuddle. 'You nearly gave me a heart attack.'

Rags started to bark his head off.

'Oh, no,' whispered Peter. 'Try to get him to stop barking. If the smugglers are there they'll be after him – and they'll find us.'

But it was too late. Rags slipped out of Miranda's grasp and was off down the passageway, still barking. He was heading for the light.

The three pelted down the last stretch of passage towards the light. Rounding the corner Peter stopped suddenly and the girls bumped into him.

'Lucy!' said Peter.

Holly and Miranda squeezed round him. The passage opened up into a little room. They stood looking at the little girl. She was sitting up in a camp-bed, blankets tumbled about her. Her face was buried in Rags's neck. She looked up and Holly saw that her face was stained with tears. Then she smiled.

'It's you!' she said. She looked at Rags. 'Oh, clever Rags,' she said, hugging him. 'You've brought them to rescue me.'

Peter, Holly and Miranda looked at one another. What on earth was going on?

Holly moved towards the camp-bed and crouched down beside it. There was a battery lamp on a box beside the bed.

'Lucy,' she said gently, 'how did you get here?'

Lucy looked up. 'Jordan brought me,' she said. 'And another man. Jordan called him Blake. They woke me up. They said if I called out they would hurt Rags.' She looked at the little terrier. 'Rags barked and Jordan kicked him. Then he put a muzzle over his mouth.'

'So I *did* hear something after all,' Holly said. 'It wasn't just the storm. It was Rags.'

'Then they brought me down here,' said Lucy. Her eyes were big. 'I was scared.'

'Oh, you poor thing,' said Miranda, putting an arm round the little girl's shoulders.

'But I had Rags with me,' she said.

'What happened then?' said Peter.

Lucy swung her legs over the bed. She was still in her pyjamas and dressing-gown. 'They said Daddy would have to pay a lot of money to get me back,' she said.

Holly, Peter and Miranda looked at one another.

'Kidnapping!' Peter said.

'*That's* why Mr Allenbury had to go to Exeter in such a hurry,' Miranda said.

'To get the ransom money,' Holly said.

'No wonder he made up that story about Lucy being in Polperro,' said Peter.

Miranda nodded. 'He would be too scared to tell anybody in case Lucy was harmed.'

Lucy was speaking again. 'And they said if I made a noise or tried to escape they would kill Rags.'

Tears began to slide down her cheeks and Miranda gave her another cuddle.

Lucy wiped her tears away with the back of her hand. 'I got that horrid muzzle off but Rags started to bark. So I had to get him away from here,' she said. She looked up at them, smiling. 'And now Rags has brought you so everything is going to be all right.'

Peter looked at the girls and raised his eyebrows.

'Of course everything is going to be all right,' said Holly.

'But how did you get Rags out?' said Miranda.

'And why couldn't you get out too?' said Peter.

Lucy jumped up from the bed. 'I'll show you,' she said.

She skipped across the room to the other

side with Rags at her heels. The passageway continued beyond the little room.

Holly, Peter and Miranda followed her.

'Mr Allenbury must have been coming back with the ransom just now,' Peter said.

'I feel awful, suspecting him,' said Miranda.

Holly nodded. 'So do I,' she said. 'But the way he behaved this morning was pretty suspicious.'

'Anyway, we have to get Lucy out of here and stop Mr Allenbury paying that ransom,' said Peter.

'Here's the place,' Lucy called to them.

Holly, Peter and Miranda stopped behind her and stared. A heavy wooden door barred the passageway. There was a rough handle on the inside of it. Peter took hold of it and tugged.

'It's locked,' he said. 'It won't move.'

Holly looked at Lucy, puzzled.

'Was the door open before?' she said. But then why would Lucy still be here?

Lucy shook her head and bent down. 'There's a space here,' she said.

Holly, Peter and Miranda bent to look. Below the door, the stone slabs had given way and there was a small opening.

'I made Rags go,' Lucy said. 'He didn't want to, but I pushed him through.'

'It must come out at the cove where we found Rags,' Holly said.

'But we didn't see a door,' Miranda said.

Peter thought for a moment. 'No,' he said. 'But that part of the cliff is full of caves. There was one just above where we found Rags.'

'And the kidnappers have their boat there,' said Miranda.

'For the getaway,' said Holly.

'Look,' said Peter. 'We've got to get out of here.' He looked at the heavy wooden door. 'That way is impossible.'

'So it's back the way we came,' said Holly.

Miranda shivered. 'I just hope we can open that secret door from the inside,' she said.

'What's that?' said Peter.

Holly listened. She thought she could hear voices coming from the other side of the door. Then the space below the door was flooded with light – torches.

'That's Jordan's voice,' Miranda said.

'And the other man,' said Holly.

Lucy looked up at them, Rags in her arms. Her eyes were trusting.

But what could they do? The kidnappers were on the other side of the door. In a moment they would find the Mystery Kids.

Kids on the run

'Come on!' said Peter. 'Back the way we came.'

Holly grabbed Lucy's hand as Rags jumped out of her arms and began scrabbling at the door.

Miranda scooped the little dog up into her arms. 'But why are they coming back?' she said as they turned to run.

'They said they would bring me something to eat,' Lucy explained.

Holly began to run. Peter was already ahead. But Lucy couldn't run as fast as the rest of them and the stone floor was uneven.

Rags was barking and struggling to get out of Miranda's grasp.

'He wants to help us,' Lucy panted. 'He wants to go back and bite those bad men, don't you, Rags?'

Rags turned his head and gave a short bark. Then he started struggling again.

'Don't let him go,' Lucy said, her blue eyes anxious. 'Jordan will kick him again.'

'Here,' Miranda said to Holly as they pelted through the little room, past the camp-bed and into the passage beyond. 'Take the torch.'

Holly let go of Lucy's hand and reached out for the torch.

Rags took his chance. He gave a final twist and jumped out of Miranda's arms. Then he ran barking back the way they had come.

'Rags!' Lucy shouted and pulled her hand out of Holly's grasp. Then she was gone, racing after Rags.

Holly whirled round. 'Come back, Lucy,' she called. But the little girl paid no attention.

Holly started to run after Lucy and Rags, through the little room, past the tumbled camp-bed. She caught up with Lucy in the passage beyond. Holly saw Rags jump up at the door. Then Lucy reached him and picked him up.

'Naughty Rags,' she said.

'Lucy!' yelled Holly.

Lucy turned and began to run towards her. But she tripped on a stone slab and fell.

Holly raced towards her and helped her up, tucking Rags firmly under her arm. There was a sound and Holly's head whipped round. It was the sound of a key in the lock. The kidnappers were coming!

'Come on,' Holly said to Lucy.

She took the little girl's hand firmly in her own.

'Run, Lucy,' she said urgently. 'Run as fast as you can!'

Holly dragged Lucy along, running towards the others.

Miranda and Peter came panting back towards them just as they reached the little room.

'What happened?' said Miranda.

'No time to explain,' said Holly. 'Take Rags.'

Miranda took the dog. Behind them they could hear the door scrape open.

'Quick,' said Peter.

Holly looked at him in dismay. Lucy was stumbling.

Peter bent down and turned his back to the little girl. 'Get on,' he said. 'I'll give you a piggyback.'

Lucy climbed on to his back.

Miranda was dancing with impatience. 'We've got to hurry,' she said.

There were voices now in the passage behind them.

'You take one torch in front, Miranda,' said Peter.

'And I'll come behind with the other one,' Holly said.

Miranda made a dive for the passageway, her torchlight bouncing off walls and floor.

Peter followed with Lucy on his back and Holly brought up the rear.

Up the passage they raced. It hadn't seemed such a long way on the way down – or so steep.

'Quick,' Holly muttered under her breath.

The passageway bent round to the right and there was the long straight stretch to the secret door in the library. Holly's breath was ragged in her throat. Her heart felt as if it would burst.

She looked at the solid expanse of the secret

door. She only hoped they could open it from the inside.

There were shouts now from behind. The kidnappers had found the little room empty. Then Holly heard the sound of pounding feet. Jordan and his friend were on their trail.

Miranda reached the door first.

'Where's the handle?' she cried.

Peter panted up, letting Lucy down. He bent over, trying to get his breath back.

'Look for a lever on the inside,' Holly yelled as she spurted for the door.

'I need some light,' Miranda said urgently.

Holly trained her torch on the door, moving the light over its surface. There was no handle.

'What are we going to do?' wailed Miranda. 'There's no handle – no lever.'

Rags heard the note of despair in her voice and stopped barking. He lifted his head and licked her cheek.

'Oh, Rags,' Miranda said. 'We're done for.'

'There must be a lever or something,' said Peter, straightening up.

'There isn't,' said Miranda.

Holly's torch-beam flickered over the door again. All the time the sound behind them was getting nearer. Then she saw it – a lever near the top of the door, almost hidden by cobwebs.

'There it is,' she said, shining her torch on the lever. Peter reached up. His fingers brushed the lever. 'It's too high,' he said.

Holly turned her head. She could hear footsteps pounding along the passageway, getting closer and closer.

'Jump,' she shouted.

Peter jumped. His fingers caught the lever and dragged it down. There was a click and the door swung open slightly.

In the crack of light a huge spider hung on a thread. Peter swallowed hard.

'You're bigger than it is, Peter,' Miranda said.

'Now I know how Little Miss Muffet felt,' Peter said.

Then he pushed at the heavy door and light flooded in from the library.

'Hurry!' he yelled and shoved Miranda through the doorway. He grabbed Lucy's hand and hurtled through the doorway with her.

Holly looked back. Jordan rounded the corner of the passage. His torch shone full in her eyes.

'Holly!' yelled Peter from the library.

Holly ran.

Miranda was already pushing the heavy bookcase shut. Holly slid through the opening into the library. Rags was barking frantically and Lucy was holding on to him, stopping him from running back into the passage to attack Jordan.

The other man was behind Jordan now. Holly heaved on the bookcase, pushing it with all her strength. Jordan was only a few metres away. As the bookcase closed with a final click she saw his face, dark with anger. His mouth curled in a sneer as he lunged for the door. Then the bookcase clicked into place.

Holly turned and leaned back on it, her breath coming in great gasps. She looked at Peter.

'What are you doing?' she said.

Peter had hold of one end of the heavy library desk. 'Help me,' he said. 'If we could get out so can they. We have to wedge something against the door.'

Holly saw what he meant. The bookcase opened inwards, into the library. If they put something heavy enough in front of it, Jordan and Blake would be trapped.

'Come on, Miranda!' Holly yelled and dived for the other end of the desk.

Miranda grabbed a corner of the desk.

'Heave,' said Peter.

They dragged the desk across the floor, hauling and pushing with all their strength. Holly's arms felt as if they were coming out of their sockets. The desk inched its way across the floor. It seemed to take forever.

'One final shove,' Peter said through clenched teeth.

'One, two, three – *push!*' Miranda said.

Holly could hear muffled sounds coming from behind the bookcase wall.

'Go for it!' she yelled and the three of them gave an extra shove.

The desk skidded into place, right up against the bookcase. Jordan and his accomplice would never get out of the passage this way.

Holly turned, breathless. 'They're trapped,' she said.

'They can't get out, Rags,' Lucy said, putting her arms round Rags. 'They won't be able to hurt you now, Rags.'

But Miranda wasn't smiling.

'What's wrong?' said Holly.

Miranda pushed her hair back from her face and turned to Holly. Her cheeks were flushed with effort.

'They'll get out the other way,' she said. 'And they've got the boat waiting for them down in the cove. They'll escape.'

Holly's heart sank. In the race to trap them behind the secret door, she had completely forgotten there was another way out.

Peter leaned against the table. They could still hear muffled sounds of banging coming from the other side of the door. Then the sounds stopped.

'They've gone,' said Holly. 'They've gone back to the boat.'

Peter looked up and grinned. 'If they have, they won't get far,' he said.

Holly looked at him. He was looking really pleased with himself.

'What do you mean?' she said.

Peter put his hand in his pocket and drew out a key. 'I took this out of the ignition,' he said.

'What?' said Miranda.

Peter's grin got even wider. 'I didn't like the look of that boat. It was all ready for a getaway so I thought I'd put a spoke in their wheel.'

'Clever,' said Miranda. 'So that's what you were doing in the cave while we were finding Rags.'

'They can't start the engine,' said Peter. 'And they can't get out this way. They really are trapped.'

Holly relaxed, then she gasped. 'No, they're not,' she said. 'They can get away by the cliff path.'

Peter bit his lip. 'I'd forgotten that,' he said. 'Look, we've got to find Mr Allenbury.'

'And we've got to block off the cliff path,' said Miranda.

Holly looked at her. 'How are we going to do that?' she said.

'First, I reckon we should contact the police,' Peter said.

Holly looked at him. Find Mr Allenbury, block off the cliff path, phone the police –

116

and what did they do with Lucy mean-
time?

There was a sound and Holly turned
towards the library door. It was opening
slowly. Someone was there – but who?

10 A race against time

The library door opened and a small figure came bustling in.

'Good heavens,' said Mrs Trelawny. Then she stopped, her eyes wide.

'Lucy!' she cried. 'What are you doing here – and in your pyjamas.'

Lucy ran to her and Mrs Trelawny gathered the little girl into her arms.

She looked at the Mystery Kids. 'What's going on?' she said.

'I was kidnapped,' Lucy blurted out. 'But Rags fetched Peter and Holly and Miranda. They rescued me.'

Mrs Trelawny's mouth fell open. 'Kidnapped!' she said.

'We don't have much time to explain, Mrs Trelawny,' Peter said.

'It's Jordan,' said Holly. 'He and another man kidnapped Lucy. They told Mr Allenbury

119

he had to pay a ransom.'

'We found her,' said Miranda. 'There's a secret passage.' She pointed to the bookcase.

'Is my father back yet, Mrs Trelawny?' Peter said.

Mrs Trelawny shook her head. She looked bewildered. Peter's face fell.

'But Mr Allenbury is here,' said Holly. 'We heard his car come back earlier.'

'He was here,' said Mrs Trelawny. 'But he's gone off.'

'Gone off?' wailed Miranda. 'Gone off where?'

Mrs Trelawny's face was drawn with worry. 'Last I saw of him he was heading for the woods,' she said.

'The woods?' Holly repeated. She looked at the others.

'What on earth is he doing in the woods?' Peter asked.

'We've got to find him,' Holly said.

Mrs Trelawny shook her head. 'Oh, no you don't,' she said. 'I don't want you running round in the woods with Jordan out there somewhere. That's a job for the police.'

'Will you phone them, Mrs Trelawny? They

might not listen to us,' said Peter.

Mrs Trelawny nodded. 'Right away,' she said briskly. 'And you three wait here. Don't move!' She took Lucy by the hand and marched out of the room, Rags at her heels.

Holly, Peter and Miranda watched as Mrs Trelawny disappeared from view.

'We can't just let those kidnappers go,' said Miranda.

Holly jumped up. 'The woods,' she said. 'That's where the summer-house is.'

'And Jordan wanted us to keep away from it,' Peter said, following her line of thought.

Miranda's face lit up. 'Do you think it's the drop-off point for the ransom money?'

Peter nodded. 'Looks like it,' he said. 'Why else would he be so keen to frighten us off?'

Holly nodded. 'We got it wrong,' she said. 'It wasn't smugglers we were dealing with.'

'So he didn't want the summer-house to stash their stuff,' said Miranda.

'It must be the collecting point for the ransom,' Peter said.

'So what do we do?' asked Miranda.

Holly bit her lip. 'There's only one thing to do,' she said. 'Mrs Trelawny is phoning the police. The kidnappers can't get away by boat, so they'll have to come by the cliff path.' She turned to the other two. 'You and Peter block off the cliff path. I'll go to the summer-house and fetch Mr Allenbury.'

'If he's there,' said Peter.

Holly nodded her head firmly. 'He'll be there,' she said. 'Why else would he be going into the woods?'

But as Holly ran stumbling along the path to the summer-house she wasn't nearly so certain Mr Allenbury would be there. What if the kidnappers had already got away by the cliff path? What if they hurt Peter and Miranda? Her torch-beam lit up swaying branches. She was alone in the wood and the kidnappers might be anywhere.

Up ahead was the turning to the summer-house. She peered through the trees. No sign of a light. No sign of anything. Then there was a sound on the path in front of her and a dark shadow moved. The figure of a man loomed over her and a hand shot out and grabbed her arm.

'What on earth . . .?' a voice said.

Holly's heart missed a beat. Then she recognised Mr Allenbury's voice.

'It's me,' she said shining the torch on her face. 'Holly.'

'Holly!' exclaimed Mr Allenbury.

Holly looked up at him. His face was white with strain. He shook his head slightly. He looked puzzled.

'What on earth are you doing here?' he said.

Holly shook her head. 'There's no time to explain,' she said. 'We know about the kidnapping. We found Lucy. She's safe. She's with Mrs Trelawny. But the kidnappers will get away if we don't stop them. You've got to come with me.'

For a moment Mr Allenbury stood there, looking at her. His face was as still as a statue's. Then Holly saw relief flood over it.

'You've found her?' he said softly. 'You've found Lucy?'

Holly nodded. 'She's safe,' she repeated. 'But we've got to hurry. You've got to help us.'

Mr Allenbury looked as if he wanted to ask questions. Then he nodded and said, 'Lead the way.'

Holly turned back the way she had come, stumbling on the rough ground. Her legs felt like lead, they were so tired. Mr Allenbury put an arm under hers and steadied her.

'Can you manage?' he said.

Holly nodded. The thought of Miranda and Peter up against Jordan and his sidekick gave her new strength.

It was comforting to have somebody as big and reliable as Mr Allenbury there. Holly remembered how relieved he looked when she told him Lucy was safe. How could they ever have suspected him?

'Have you still got the ransom?' Holly asked as they hurried through the woods.

Mr Allenbury nodded. 'I was on my way to drop it off,' he said. He looked down at her and smiled gently. 'I'd like to know how you found out about all this – later,' he said.

'We'll tell you the whole story,' Holly said as they came to the turning for the cliff path. 'But right now we've got to get to the cliff path. Peter and Miranda are trying to block Jordan's escape.'

'Jordan?' said Mr Allenbury.

Holly turned to look at him. Of course, he wouldn't know who the kidnappers were.

'And another man,' said Holly.

They were out of the woods now, running

for the cliff path. They could hear shouts and yells in the distance.

Holly heard Peter yell out. She gritted her teeth and forced her tired legs to run faster. Then she could see two figures at the top of the path down to the cove.

'There they are!' she shouted.

Peter turned as they came up. 'Thank goodness you're here,' he said. 'Get some more rocks and stones.'

Holly and Mr Allenbury looked at him.

'Take that!' Miranda yelled, hurling a large rock two-handed down the narrow cliff path. There was a yell of pain from below.

'Say no more,' said Mr Allenbury and, turning, picked up a rock that none of the children could have lifted. He sent it hurtling down the path.

There was the most amazing rumble as the rock gathered speed. Then the sounds of shouts and yells and feet running. Then there was the sound of cries and bodies falling.

'Wow!' said Peter. 'That's stopped them.'

Mr Allenbury dusted off his hands. 'Let's go and pick up the pieces, shall we?' he said.

Holly looked at him. His face was stern.

She didn't fancy being in Jordan's shoes when Mr Allenbury got hold of him.

She put out a hand. 'Mr Allenbury,' she said, 'the police will be here soon. Shouldn't we wait for them?'

For a moment, she thought Mr Allenbury hadn't heard her. Then he raised a hand to his head and looked down at her.

'Maybe you're right,' he said. 'I don't know if I could trust myself if I got my hands on Jordan.'

'Look!' said Peter.

Headlights pierced the night sky and the sound of car engines came to them.

'The police,' Miranda said. 'I'll go and fetch them. You wait here in case those two try to make a run for it.'

Holly looked at Miranda. Her clothes were torn and dirty. Her face was covered in dust and her hair was all over the place. But her eyes were shining with triumph. Holly grinned at her and Miranda grinned back.

'Not that I think they *will* try to make a run for it,' she said. 'But you never know your luck.' She handed Holly a rock. 'If you hear them coming back, just chuck that down,' she said.

Then she was off, racing down the path towards the house, waving her torch and shouting.

Holly, Peter and Mr Allenbury stood guarding the top of the path. They could hear Miranda's voice in the distance calling to the police, leading them across the lawns.

'How did you find out about the kidnapping?' Mr Allenbury said.

'We didn't know it was kidnapping,' said Peter.

'At first we thought Jordan and Blake were smugglers,' Holly said.

'Blake?' Mr Allenbury said sharply.

Holly nodded. 'Lucy said that's what Jordan called the other man.'

'Do you know him?' Peter asked.

Mr Allenbury nodded. 'He was odd-job man here. I had to dismiss him for stealing.'

'So then he turned kidnapper,' said Holly.

Mr Allenbury shook his head. 'I thought Jordan was mixed up in the thefts as well but I couldn't prove it. I didn't have enough evidence. And you can't just dismiss a man on suspicion. He wasn't even any good as a gardener. I put him on a last warning.'

Holly remembered the conversation Mr

Allenbury had with Jordan on the lawns –
just before he went to Exeter.

'Was that why Jordan was so angry yesterday?' she said.

Mr Allenbury nodded. 'That and the fact
that I told him to stay away from the house.'

'So the two of them decided to get their
revenge on you,' said Peter.

'It looks like it,' said Mr Allenbury. 'But to
do that to Lucy . . .' His voice trailed off as
he turned away.

Holly and Peter looked at each other. The
same thought was in both their minds. How
could they have suspected Mr Allenbury?

Miranda's voice was nearer now.

'Over here,' she called.

Holly and Peter turned. Miranda was leading a group of policemen towards them.
Torches shone in the darkness and then
the policemen were beside them, asking
questions, taking over.

One of the policemen stepped forward.

'Sergeant Watkins,' said Mr Allenbury.

Sergeant Watkins was a round-faced,
kindly looking man.

'I think we've got most of the story out of
this young lady,' he said to Mr Allenbury.

Mr Allenbury smiled. 'We've got a lot to thank these three for,' he said.

Sergeant Watkins looked at Holly and Peter and smiled. 'Just you stand back now and let my men get on with the job. We don't want anybody hurt if those two decide to put up a fight.' He turned to his men. 'Right, lads,' he said. 'Let's get on with it.'

He stood at the top of the path, his men round him.

'This is the police,' he shouted. 'We don't want any more trouble. Just come quietly and nobody will get hurt.'

There was a silence. Holly held her breath. Then she heard voices muttering and arguing below on the cliff path. There was another silence before the sound of feet on the path. Sergeant Watkins nodded to two of his men and they started down the cliff path to meet Jordan and Blake.

In fact Jordan and Blake weren't in any condition to put up a fight. The policemen led the two men up the path; Jordan was limping badly and the other man had a cut on his forehead.

As Jordan passed, he looked at Holly, Peter and Miranda.

'If only you kids hadn't come down here,' he said. 'I knew you were trouble the minute I saw you.'

Mr Allenbury took a step towards him and Jordan flinched. Holly saw Mr Allenbury's fists curl into balls.

Then Sergeant Watkins said, 'We'll deal with this, sir. You go on back to the house. You'll want to see your daughter. And we'll need to talk to her.'

At the mention of Lucy, Mr Allenbury's face changed.

'Lucy!' he said. 'She'll be wondering where I am. You're right. I must go to her.'

'I'll be right behind you,' said Sergeant Watkins. 'Just as soon as I've got these two packed off to the police station.'

Mr Allenbury watched the two men being led away. He turned to Holly and the other two.

'I don't know what to say,' he began.

'Oh,' said Miranda airily. 'It was nothing. It's all in a day's work for the Mystery Kids.'

Mr Allenbury looked puzzled but Holly took his arm. 'Lucy was worried about you,' she said.

At once Mr Allenbury was on his way, striding out towards the house.

'Come on, then,' said Peter. He looked at the girls. Their hair was tangled and dirty, their clothes were filthy. 'You two look terrible,' he said.

Holly and Miranda exchanged a look and burst out laughing. 'And what do you think you look like?' said Miranda.

Peter grinned. 'Just think, we could have got all dressed up to go out with Dad tonight.'

'Your dad!' said Miranda. 'What on earth is he going to think if he comes back to find the place surrounded by policemen?'

Peter shrugged. 'He's getting used to our adventures,' he said.

Holly laughed. 'Maybe he is,' she said. 'But I'd rather be there when he arrives. We'll have to do a bit of explaining.'

Miranda looked down at her torn and dirty shorts. 'And maybe get cleaned up?' she said.

'Come on,' said Peter.

The front door of the house came into view. Light flooded from every window.

131

Mr Allenbury was framed in the doorway with Lucy in his arms. Mrs Trelawny was standing beside them. She was carrying a golf club. She had obviously been ready to defend Lucy against Jordan and Blake. Rags was leaping around, barking excitedly.

'Mrs Trelawny was ready for the kidnappers,' said Holly.

Miranda giggled. 'What a night!' she said.

There was a crunch on the gravel behind them and a voice said, 'What's going on?'

Peter turned. 'Oh, hello, Dad,' he said. 'Had a good evening?'

Mr Hamilton looked his son over from the top of his tangled head to his scraped and dirty trainers.

'Never mind my evening,' he said. 'What are all these police cars doing here? Has there been an accident? Are you all right?'

Peter smiled. 'We're fine, Dad. Honest.'

Mr Hamilton looked relieved. 'You'd better tell me what's happened,' he said. 'I hope you three haven't been getting up to any mischief while I've been away.'

Holly, Peter and Miranda laughed.

'You wouldn't believe it, Dad,' he said.

'I probably would,' Mr Hamilton said ruefully. 'That's the trouble.'

Holly looked at him. 'Everything's all right now,' she said.

Mr Hamilton looked at them. 'Why do I worry whenever you say that?' he said.

Holly laughed. 'Oh, you mustn't,' she said. 'You mustn't worry about the Mystery Kids. We always come out on top.'

She looked towards the front door of Greystones. Mr Allenbury was hugging Lucy as if he would never let her go. And Rags was leaping round Mr Allenbury's legs. The little terrier was barking his head off again. But this time it wasn't in fear and anger. This time Rags was barking for joy.

Another Hodder Children's book

Fiona Kelly

SPY-CATCHERS!
THE MYSTERY KIDS 1

You can't keep a secret from these three!

London is teeming with spies –
and Holly and Miranda are just the
people to catch them.

All they need is practice. Who is the
sinister man lurking outside Holly's
house? What does Miranda's mother
really do for the government?

Then they spot a suspicious-
looking boy – and the real mystery
begins . . .

Another Hodder Children's book

Fiona Kelly

**LOST AND FOUND
THE MYSTERY KIDS 2**

A ticket to adventure

Holly's desperate for a mystery to
solve – and when she sees a ferrety-
looking man throw his wallet from
the bus, she knows she's found one!

Peter and Miranda aren't so sure.
The wallet is empty when they go
back to find it. Empty except for
some sort of ticket – and there's
nothing mysterious about that . . . or
is there?

h HODDER

Another Hodder Children's book

Fiona Kelly

TREASURE HUNT
THE MYSTERY KIDS 3

On the trail of a lost fortune

What happens when you've got
no crime to solve? You look for an
unsolved crime!

The Mystery Kids read about a
blackmail attempt that happened
years earlier. The criminal was
arrested – but the money was never
found! Now Holly, Miranda and
Peter are in pursuit of a suitcase full
of cash.

Trouble is, the Mystery Kids aren't
the only ones looking . . .

Another Hodder Children's book

Fiona Kelly

**THE EMPTY HOUSE
THE MYSTERY KIDS 4**

A mystery in your back garden!

There's something strange going on in the empty house behind Peter's new home. The Mystery Kids decide to take a look – and discover that it's not abandoned after all!

Now they are on the trail of some very nasty criminals . . .

THE MYSTERY KIDS SERIES
Fiona Kelly